WHAT PEOPLE ARE SAYING ABOUT

THE LIVES OF THE APOSTATES

I've long been an admirer of ⌐ ....ism. His stories are so smart, so we.................................... ...... ⌐ learn that he would be publishing a nov................................... .g read it in one sitting, I'm glad Scott's writing ....ction," too. Only, *The Lives of the Apostates* is more than that – at its best, it's a complication of belief and beliefs, the story of a clash between a student and a professor, between religion and reality, between a young man's faith and his circumstances.

Jeff Sharlet, bestselling author of *The Family* and *Sweet Heaven When I Die*

Finally, something new under the sun: a midwestern pagan coming of age story that is at once a poignant evocation of young love and a searing meditation on the ancient conflict between faiths. As sharp as a ritual blade, as full as a chalice, *The Lives of the Apostates* is a great surprise, and Eric Scott a writer to watch.

Peter Manseau, author of *Songs for the Butcher's Daughter* and *Rag and Bone*

Eric Scott's *The Lives of the Apostates* is a tone poem of rage and grief at growing up in a world where your very beliefs place you in opposition to the way most of the world is run, to the blunt instruments of religious power and privilege. Scott is a lyrical and powerful essayist whose foray into fiction echoes the very real lives of the apostates among us, and within us. A barbaric yawp from the Pagan soul.

Jason Pitzl-Waters, blogger, *The Wild Hunt: A Modern Pagan Perspective*

Drawing on his own life experience, Eric Scott allows us to perceive the world through the eyes of a second generation Pagan. *The Lives of the Apostates* is a gritty tale of culture clash, reconciliation and unrequited love. Scott has a talent for creating characters who are neither heroes nor true villains, but rather realistic people with their own strengths and flaws.

Alaric Albertsson, author, *Travels Through Middle Earth: The Path of a Saxon Pagan*

The Lives
of the
Apostates

The Lives
of the
Apostates

Eric O. Scott

Winchester, UK
Washington, USA

First published by Moon Books, 2013
Moon Books is an imprint of John Hunt Publishing Ltd., Laurel House, Station Approach,
Alresford, Hants, SO24 9JH, UK
office1@jhpbooks.net
www.johnhuntpublishing.com
www.moon-books.net

For distributor details and how to order please visit the 'Ordering' section on our website.

Text copyright: Eric O. Scott 2012

ISBN: 978 1 78099 910 4

A CIP catalogue record for this book is available from the British Library.

Design: Stuart Davies

Printed in the USA by Edwards Brothers Malloy

We operate a distinctive and ethical publishing philosophy in all
areas of our business, from our global network of authors to
production and worldwide distribution.

For Sarah,
sister, muse, lavender fairy

"The world has always warmed to its fallen heroes. Hector rather than Achilles, Robert E. Lee and not Ulysses S. Grant, stir the imagination of posterity, however lost or wrong-headed the causes they championed. They fill the Valhalla of our fantasies. The emperor Julian is in a similar class. The wonder of historian and artist is still aroused by the late-Roman prince, nephew of Constantine, who lived his early years in constant peril of sharing his father's fate, his youth in almost total isolation, and his early manhood as a wandering and dreaming student. Yet he almost overnight turned into a born leader, and an administrator who bent every effort during a reign of twenty months in a hopeless effort to restore the old religion. His death in battle at the age of thirty-two in a grandiose scheme to conquer the Persian Empire and emulate Alexander the Great seems only to add stature to what objectively was a wasteful and futile endeavor."

-W.H.C. Frend, *The Rise of Christianity*

I

I have this fantasy about throwing a brick through the window of the House of Jesus. I want to see it buckle in, want to watch the shards of glass rain down among the aisles of inspirational books and Precious Moments figures. I want to hear the music, like frenzied wind chimes, as the pane falls onto the wooden floor. I want to laugh like a Viking setting fire to a monastery. And then I want to run like hell.

I can't decide whether I would steal anything or not. It seems like I ought to. Destruction for the sake of destruction seems petty, but thievery still has a little romance to it. You can still sympathize with a burglar. But there's nothing at a Christian supply store for me, and I wouldn't want to take something I had no use for.

I would never actually do this, of course. I'd get caught. Kirksville, the town where I go to college, is too small to get away with anything like that. Maybe on graduation night, when everybody's distracted... But probably not even then.

Still. It might be worth it.

I remember this one time, in my sophomore year, when I was driving through the town square and saw the clerk from the House of Jesus struggling with a package. She's an older woman with roller-tight auburn curls. She had a FedEx package in her hands – a big, monstrous thing. She could barely lift it. I stopped my car and jumped out to help her. The labels said it was full of copies of *The Purpose Driven Life*.

I hefted that package, and I had this thought: I could take that box of books, these books that were full of pabulum and conde-scension, and I could run off with them. Throw them into the alley, maybe, or jump back in my car, drive to campus, and abandon them in the basement of Baldwin Hall. Anything to get rid of them, to deprive the House of Jesus of its best seller.

But I didn't do that. I pussed out and carted the box inside, asked the old woman where she wanted the box to go. She pointed me to another stack of Rick Warren books and thanked me for being such a kind young man.

I don't know why, when given the chance, I didn't take it. I could have gotten away with the box, I think – she's an old woman, slow, bad eyes. Then again, I don't know why I have the urge in the first place. I guess it's to prove a point, but I couldn't tell you what that point is.

Anyway, that was a year ago. Right now it's late August. The freshmen will be arriving next weekend in their droves, crowding the streets and the sidewalks, slavering at their first taste of college independence. For the moment, though, Kirksville was quiet. Nobody walked through the steaming summer heat except townies and the few students who stayed over between semesters, like me. The summer had dragged. Nobody to talk to, no parties to attend. Nothing to do but go to work and then come home to an apartment without air conditioning.

I turned onto Scott Street and headed up to a complex of generic buildings – half a dozen of them, so similar that only the address numbers tell them apart. A wooden sign out front read "CHERITON VALLEY". I parked and headed to building 3A.

Before I could get my keys out to unlock the door, I heard heavy metal playing from the television inside. I rubbed my forehead and opened the door. This was a bad omen for the night to come.

The living room, clinical white and covered in a thin lair of dust, held three men. Two of them were sitting; the third jumped up and down in a frenzy.

Mike, my counterpart, sat in a tan armchair staring at the television. Mike was one of the few black guys native to Kirksville. He was a couple of years older than me, 27 or 28. He had a body like a scarecrow: incredibly tall and impossibly thin.

"Hey Lou," he said. "You're early."

"I thought I'd come in and get my paperwork done."

I looked at the television and saw two huge, sweaty men in underwear grappling, confirming my suspicions: the heavy metal had been Stone Cold Steve Austin's entrance music.

The boys (I shouldn't call them *boys*, I should call them *mentally-handicapped-adults*, but I can't help it) loved pro wrestling. Or at least Donny – who at the moment was screaming, "Un-der-taker! Un-der-taker!" – he loved pro wrestling. He demanded to watch every WWE show we could get on Cheriton's basic cable plan, even the crappy Sunday night show that never had any big name wrestlers on it, and when no show was on, he had eight wrestling tapes that he played again and again.

Jimmy was the other resident of the house. He was an older guy, though I didn't know exactly how old – forties, maybe – with thick glasses and a gray beard we had to keep cut for him. He sat on the couch, staring into space. I don't know that Jimmy *liked* anything. I'm not sure Jimmy was high-functioning enough to understand joy.

I grimaced at the tape. "Hey, Mike. Can I talk to you for a sec?"

"Sure." Mike didn't stand up so much as he unfolded from the chair, raising up to nearly six and a half feet. We walked out of the white-and-beige living room into the white-and-beige kitchen. "What's up?"

"It's eight o'clock," I said in a whisper. "Why the fuck are they watching wrestling?"

"Donny wanted to watch his Undertaker tape. He wouldn't shut up about it." He looked at the television, then back at me. "It's almost over, I promise."

I glanced over to see a Hell in a Cell match from the late '90s – the kind where they put a big cage around the ring that looks to be made of spools of aluminum fencing. The Undertaker choke-slammed his opponent, Mankind, through the top of the cage and down to the ring, some twenty feet below. Mankind would lay there for a few minutes, unconscious, with a broken tooth up his nose. Then he would get up again despite the screams of the announcers to stay down. Eventually they'd call in a stretcher, and then he would bust off of that, too. I knew the entire sequence by heart. I'd been forced to watch this tape about twelve times already.

"Jesus Christ," I muttered. "It just gets him all wound up. He's supposed to go to bed in an hour and a half."

"He'll calm down. Seriously, Lou, he would have been more aggravating if I hadn't put it on. Kid loves his Undertaker." The 'kid' was in his thirties, years older than either of us, but, like I said – it's hard not to think of them that way.

"Yeah, yeah. I know. Putting him to bed's going to be hell, but oh well." I shrugged. The boys had given me worse nights. "Anyway. I've got my paperwork."

"Let me know when you get done so I can start mine."

I was essentially a baby-sitter, especially on the midnight shift. I made sure the boys didn't hurt themselves, that they got fed and took their pills, that they got a healthy amount of sleep. Given those responsibilities, the paperwork always struck me as unreasonable. There was a form for clocking in, another for clocking out, a timetable for meals, a timetable for meds. There was the minor incident form – I had to use that one once, when Donny tripped over an end table and twisted his ankle. There's a major incident form, too, but I never had to use that one. And there were more forms than those, too – reimbursement forms and the like, for when we took the boys out for groceries, things like that.

I filled out my clock-in sheet and initialed the meal timetable. I looked up towards the living room. "They had dinner, Mike?"

"Yessir," he said, his gaze on the TV. "Finest SpaghettiOs in the state of Missouri."

Jimmy briefly stirred at the mention of SpaghettiOs, but once he realized we weren't about to cook anything, he went back into his usual catatonia.

I finished my beginning-of-shift duties and went back into the den. "All yours, chief."

"You have the bridge, Number One," he said, and went to the kitchen to start filling out his sheets. It took him about ten minutes, during which time approximately three minutes and wrestling and seven minutes of commentary flashed by. I heard him close up the paperwork binder and slide it back onto the shelf. He walked back into the living room and waved goodbye to the boys and me. "See you guys on Tuesday."

"Not working tomorrow?" I asked.

"I haven't taken my girl out in a month, man. I'm taking the night off before she stabs me."

"Right on," I said, and immediately hated myself for saying it. It sounded like the kind of thing a lame middle-class white boy would say, and I hate to admit the truth about myself. "Have fun, man."

He opened the door, gave us a last wave, and left.

"Bye Mike!" Donny yelled.

Jimmy said nothing.

* * *

I got Donny to sleep around ten o'clock, much later than he should have been in bed. We argued for an hour over a wrestling move called the Tombstone Piledriver, and whether it belonged to the Undertaker or his 'brother', Kane. (At least I think it was an argument. It's hard to tell with the boys.) In the end we agreed that the move belonged to both of them, but 'Taker used it first.

Usually it wouldn't have mattered much if Donny stayed up, but he was high-functioning enough that the company had gotten him a job at the Ponderosa Steakhouse, so he needed to be up early for that. Unfortunately, that also meant I had no company for the rest of the night. The boredom was the worst part of overnights. The boys weren't scintillating conversationalists, but at least they gave me something to do; once they were in bed, my job consisted of not falling asleep until six AM. Thankfully, we traded overnights every few weeks, so I didn't have to do that all the time.

Mostly I watched TV. I became acquainted with the slow drift from the end of primetime into late-night news and talk shows, which eventually dissolved into the faerie country between two and five AM. I had watched too many infomercials for strange kitchen appliances and seen too many evangelistic pleas from megachurches in my time at Cheriton Valley. At least when the semester started, I could do homework to pass the time.

I sank into the easy chair and flipped the channel over to *The Daily Show*. Funny, but forgettable – some Bush gaffes, a segment with the bald guy 'on assignment' in South Carolina.

I itched for someone to talk to. At the commercial break I started to look through my phone, trying to think of somebody to call. Names scrolled past: Kyle Favazza, Tony Lacey, Mikayla Plinkett. A whole repository of relationships, sorted by ringtones and thumbnails. People I hadn't talk to in years, people I'd probably never talk to again, but at some point, had been important to me. I couldn't bring myself to delete them.

Hailey Thomas... Alan Von Alman...

Lucy Walstead.

A photograph flashed next to the name, a smiling girl with turquoise hair. You might have mistaken it for a wig, but only if you didn't know her.

I sent her a text. *Hey. You busy?*

About a minute later, I got a reply. *Not really. What's up?*

I hit the call button and muted the TV. Garbled closed-captions appeared. *IT'S A WONDERFUL IDEA*, the captions informed me long after Jon Stewart's lips had formed the punchline, *EXCEPT FOR THE PART WHERE IT DOESN'T*

WORK.

"Hello?" said Lucy, her voice tinny over the phone.

"Hey, kid. How are you?" I asked.

"It's a little late for you to be calling, isn't it?" She yawned. "Don't you have class?"

"Not until next week. Anyway, I'm working tonight."

"Oh, right. Night shift, huh?" Lucy always sounds like she's talking in her sleep: her voice, high and quiet, full of strange lilts and musical notes. "That must be rough."

"I've been doing it for a little while now. Eventually you forget what the sun looks like, and then it's not so bad."

She chuckled. "How's the semester look?"

"Okay, I think." I paused, trying to remember my schedule. "Mostly major classes… Logic should be interesting; it's got a good professor. The only one I'm dreading is History of Christian Thought."

"You're taking Christian Thought?" she asked. "Really?"

"Blame the dean. It's a major requirement. Or at least, something from the Abrahamic religions is, and every other class that fits the requirement starts at seven in the morning. It's that Protestant work-ethic for you."

I pictured her nodding on the other end of the line. (The line that doesn't exist anymore because we're using cell phones. Yes, I know. Look, language has some catching up to do.) "Lou Durham in a course on Christian Thought. I never thought I'd see the day." She paused. "That's got to be a short textbook."

We both went silent, and then at once burst into laughter.

"That's terrible," I said, once I had caught my breath. "And you're a terrible person for saying it."

"You laughed."

"I never said I wasn't a terrible person too."

She chuckled. "Well, good luck, I guess. What's the plan? Sit in the back, try not to fall asleep?"

"Miss Walstead, you offend my honor as an academic and a

scholar," I said. "I intend to confront these ideas from a position of cautious respect and thoroughly interrogate them as a student of comparative religion ought to approach any system."

"Uh huh."

"...from the back row, while doing the crossword."

"That's my boy." She paused. "The whole history? That's a lot of time to cover in one semester."

"Nah, it's just the first section. I think there's three in all? This one just goes up to the beginning of the Middle Ages... 600, 700, something like that."

"The Romans, basically. Well, hey, there'll be some neat people in there, at least. Hypatia, maybe? And the Emperor Julian, he's got to have a chapter or two dedicated to him."

"Yeah, I'm really looking forward reading about how the last Pagan emperor fucks up and dies, Lucy. That's going to be a laugh a minute."

"It's better than old men excommunicating each other."

"Root canals fit that description."

I hadn't talked to Lucy in months – not since June, when my parents held the Midsummer sabbat at our house in St. Louis. We had all made it to that one, for once – me, Lucy, her brother Andy, and our friend Dottie – the little tribe of Pagan children who had grown up together in our parents' coven. We almost never all made into town for the sabbats anymore. Mostly that could be blamed on distance – Lucy lived in Madison now, studying Linguistics, and I lived here in Kirksville. Dottie and Andy still lived in St. Louis, but neither of them went to many festivals. Not since they broke up. I guess they both worried they'd die of awkwardness if they had to stand next to each other for an hour.

Lucy wore a white robe at Midsummer, cotton, and when the wind blew I could see the nubs of her breasts push against the fabric. We stood next to each other in circle, like we always have, ever since we were little kids. We held hands and watched my mother and father drawing figures in the salt and the water, invoking the elements and the gods, blessing the wine and the cakes. I can picture every detail: our overgrown yard, drenched in sunlight and greenery, and Lucy's violet hair catching a glimmer of the Sun God's glory.

I can think of my life as a succession of pictures like this, a parade of Lucy Walsteads that stretches back into the darkness of youth. Lucy at eight, dressed in magenta for Beltane, her hair still blonde; Lucy at 14, standing with me at Samhain in a deep emerald dress, the first time she dyed her hair Tinkerbelle green. Lucy at 21, in my parents' yard, tall and violet-haired and beautiful beyond words.

I had watched her grow up, from a little girl to the radiant Valkyrie I saw at Midsummer, and I had grown up with her, starting squat and short, becoming taller and broader and hairier. And I held her hand all the while.

She wore a white robe that day, the last time I held her hand, the last time I'd passed her a chalice and a plate of home-made bread. The last time I had wished that she would never thirst and never hunger, that I had kissed her and tasted the white wine of the Goddess.

"Are you going home for Harvest?" she asked.

"I don't know. Probably. I hadn't really thought about it…" I heard a noise from the boys' room. "Hey, Luce, hold on a minute."

"Sure. Is something wrong?"

"Not sure. I'll be right back."

I sat my phone down and walked down the hall to the bedrooms, but before I got there, Jimmy stumbled out. He had taken off his pajamas, and stood in the middle of the hallway, naked and hairy. He looked right past me, as though I weren't there, and then kept walking. I let him by. According to the law, I can't touch either of them; if they want to do something, the best I can do is try to talk them out of it. I can't physically restrain the boys. And, frankly, I knew the kinds of shit Jimmy got into sometimes. I didn't really want to touch him, though sometimes, I wished I'd had the option.

"Hey, buddy," I said. "Come on, get back in your room. It's late."

He walked to the front door and took a few steps out into the parking lot. Just what I needed: Jimmy walking around Kirksville naked on my watch. I followed him out into the chilly autumn air. He stopped at the edge of the sidewalk and look up at the moon.

"Jimmy, come on. You'll catch a cold. Come on back inside, buddy."

He didn't move; Mother Luna had entranced him, and he stood there with his arms slack at his side, staring up. God, what I would have given just to grab him by the shoulders and drag him inside... Instead I found myself stepping up next to him and looking up too, hoping that none of the other caretakers saw us.

I looked at Jimmy. He had a wide vacant face and a scraggly beard and pockmarks all over his body. Most of the time, he just sat on the couch and did nothing at all, but occasionally he got urges like this one and couldn't be dissuaded from them. He was different from Donny; Donny could be reasoned with, to a point. Donny understood when I told him to do something. He might argue, he might rebel, but he understood.

Not Jimmy. Jimmy had his silent life and his occasional mystic compulsions, like the time we took the boys to the carnival and he'd stayed on the Tilt-A-Whirl for an hour, refusing to budge an inch when he was told his turn was over and he had to go. Jimmy almost never wanted anything, but when he did, by God, he wanted it with the totality of his being.

I put my hand on his shoulder, knowing that I was breaking the rules, and patted him gently. "Come on, buddy. It's cold out here. Let's go in."

For a second I felt him tense up like a brick wall, but then he turned soft, and he let me walk him back into the house. I led him to his room, where, to my horror and vindication, I discovered he'd shit his pajamas. I dressed him in another pair and carried the dirty ones out to the washing machine.

It took me twenty minutes, all told, to get back to the phone. By then, Lucy had hung up, of course. She'd left a message: *Sorry, champ, my classes do start tomorrow. Give me a call when you aren't on the night shift, we'll find something good and schlocky on cable. Love, bb, Lucy.*

The boys weren't awake yet when Dana arrived. Dana's my boss, sort of – she doesn't sign the checks, but she's the house supervisor, so she looks over the paperwork and makes sure our crew doesn't neglect the boys.

I don't talk to her much. I mean, why would I? We had nothing in common. She grew up in Macon, forty minutes south of Kirksville, has two kids, got divorced when she was 38. She's been working for Cheriton Valley for seventeen years. Me, I grew up in the city; I read about David Hume and epistemology. Dana is who I don't want to end being when I'm 45: prudent, and quiet, and not disappointed with her life. I want to be reckless. I want to be loud. I want to be constantly disappointed. I looked forward to disappointment the way a worker looks forward to quitting time.

* * *

I heard the low mumble of television on the other side of my apartment door when I got home that morning. It was about 6:35 AM, and from the noise's steady rhythm, I guessed that the morning news was on. I walked in and glanced at the television; a sour-faced news anchor confirmed my suspicion. Something else to list in my daily accomplishments.

My roommate sat on the couch, reading a book by lamplight. He wore the same clothes had been wearing when I left for work last night: black cargo pants, black combat boots, a black t-shirt that informed the world that MY INVISIBLE FRIENDS THINK

YOU'RE CRAZY. Silver chains everywhere. He didn't look up when I entered the room; he flipped a page and adjusted his thick glasses, not diverting his attention for a moment.

"Hey, Grimey," I said, and locked the door. "Up early, aren't you?"

"I never went to bed," he said. Grimey flipped some of his long, oily hair out of his face. I worry about his hair. Sometimes I think I should do what my Aunt Mabel did and put plastic sheets on the couch to protect them from grease stains. (It is *my* couch, after all. I paid for it and hauled it in myself. I think Grimey might have bought his own office chair, but I wouldn't swear to it.) "I've been up reading this book."

"What book is it?"

He raised the cover to me: a psychedelic scene of a green-skinned man bearing a sword, ascending from the metallic corpse of some kind of robot. A sharp crease slid down the left side of the paperback. I recognized the author immediately: Robert Anton Wilson, one of my favorite maniacs.

"Hey! *Prometheus Rising!* That's a great book."

"Mm-hmm," he said, his eyes still fixed on the page.

"I wonder what I did with my copy."

"This is your copy, Lou. You loaned it to me."

"What?" I asked. "When?"

"Uhm. A little while ago." Grimey can be frustratingly laconic. He doesn't do it to be evasive, not intentionally – usually – but it's damned annoying. His answer to any question involving time is 'a while'. "Right before we moved out of the dorms, I think."

"Are you telling me you've had my book for, what, a year and a half now?"

"Well," he said, "you never asked for it back..."

I gave the crease on the cover an evil stare. "Put it back when you're done."

I needed to catch a nap, at least, or maybe even a full day's sleep, but Grimey turned a corner on the page he was reading –

bastard! – and spoke up again. "You remember this quarter experiment Wilson talks about? The one where you're supposed to, like, visualize a quarter, in your mind's eye? And do it really hard? Then you go out and look for the quarter you pictured, to see if it's real?"

"Sure. What about it?"

"Did you ever try it?"

"Nah. Never tried most of the stuff in that book," I said. "I think Bob Wilson's a good philosopher, but I got the idea, you know? All that stuff about your mind being able to affect reality, how you filter out all the things you aren't expecting to see, that kind of shit." I shrugged. "The quarter thing is kind of a weak example. It doesn't work in real life."

Grimey put on a skeptical, knowing face, and nodded in the way he thinks will make me look wise. Grimey doesn't have the face for wisdom – nobody would ever confuse him for a sage. He's always struck me as a slightly underdone infant, still just a little too pink. "You're just saying that because you could never find a quarter."

"No, Grimey, I never found a quarter." I leaned against the wall, my back crinkling some poster of a metal band Grimey listened to.

"Because you didn't believe in the quarter!"

"Because people don't just abandon quarters on sidewalks! Have you ever dropped a quarter and then gone, 'meh, not like I have any use for that thing?' People stop and pick up their quarters. Best I ever did was when I found a dime, once, down by the library."

"I'm gonna try it," he said. He set the book on the coffee table. "Watch me; I'll be drowning in them before the week is out."

"And the Laundromats of the world will sing your praises, O Philosopher, for loading them with the Quarters of True Wisdom." I turned towards the bedrooms. "Look, man, I really need to catch a nap before class. We'll argue about your delusions later, alright?"

"You got it." He grinned. Grimey had excellent teeth; his mother's a dentist. "Sleep well, my friend."

"Right. Thanks."

Down the hall and to the right, that was my room. Hard to open the door all the way due to the dirty clothes on the floor. Grimey and me, we didn't live in a "responsible" way, but neither of us minded the other's slovenliness, so we got along. We met because, at Lucy's suggestion, I tried to start the Truman State Campus Pagans group in my freshmen year. Six people joined the Facebook group. Only Grimey showed up at the meeting. I never imagined that I would end up living with a man who only answers to the name 'Grimalkin', but in Kirksville, the pickings were pretty slim once you moved beyond frat boys and evangelists.

Before college, I would have called Grimey a 'K-Mart Pagan'. That's what my dad always called his kind: they picked up a book and decided witchcraft sounded like a cool hobby, so they went looking for supplies. When they had acquired enough essential oils, pentagrams, and varieties of incense, they declared themselves True Witches and began to preach the gospel. (I learned to stay out of Grimey's room early on in our friendship due to the overwhelming mixture of marijuana and Nag Champa. After negotiations, he agreed to ease up on the Nag Champa.)

He was easy to make fun of, for a kid like me, born and raised in Wicca. We could point to him – solitary, uninitiated, someone who had barely ever done a ritual – and claim that only we were the One True Pagans. But...

I looked at my altar, over in the corner of my bedroom. I've kept an altar ever since I moved away from home, but I've never been great about the upkeep. The statues of my gods – Odin, Mercury, Thoth, Athena as the token female – hadn't been dusted in months, and the wine in the little chalice had long since evaporated, leaving behind a strange honey resin that served only as a trap for fruit flies. Around the little island of gods churned a sea of dirty socks and discarded homework, and beyond that, an unmade bed and a television whose only function was to play video games.

I really should have dusted off the table, said a few prayers, made some offerings. I didn't have much to give beyond a cheap jug of white wine in the kitchen, but I always believed the gods appreciated the thought more than the materials involved. Apparently I wasn't much good at keeping the thought in mind either.

There were a lot of things I'd neglected scattered throughout my room: the piles of laundry, the stack of unreturned library books, the calendar of moon phases Andy got me for Yule. A lot of things I should have already done, and more that I still needed to do.

I should have done something, but it was seven AM and I had been awake for twenty hours. I told myself 'maybe later', but I already knew that I wouldn't.

II

I sometimes wonder if Dr. Eccleston polished his skull before he came to class. The fluorescent lights of the classroom glared off the top of his head so brightly that I could never bear to look at him for more than a few seconds. Skin shouldn't *do* that.

He was probably in his mid-fifties. His hair – what he had left, anyway – had likely been bright red at one point, but had faded to a rusty gray. He wore a mustache, but no beard. Unfortunate, that. A beard would have covered up the crater in his chin that bulged whenever he talked.

Today he wore a purple sweater, which seemed a little much for so early in the fall. I have this theory about male professors, at least here at Truman State. They come in two basic varieties: suits and sweaters. Both safe, academic garments, but they served different functions. A suit – I'm thinking of the collegiate tweed model, the kind with elbow patches – projects an aura of authority: *I'm an expert. You are not. Defer to me.* Sweaters, on the other hand – almost always knit wool, which ought to tell you something – say just the opposite: *Hey, we're all human beings here. I just happen to stand at the head of the class. Trust me.* Those are just first impressions, and they're both laced with bullshit, but you can tell a lot about a person from the first impression – mostly what kind of person he thinks he is.

Dr. Eccleston was definitely a Sweater Prof. He projected this image of paternal warmth, like your kind old uncle, except he had a doctorate in Church History. He might as well have had *Trust Me* embroidered on his chest.

"Tertullian – one of the church fathers we read about in chapter six..." He wrote the name on the board and turned to face us, juggling his chalk in his left hand. Probably an affectation. "Tertullian said that 'the blood of martyrs is the seed of church.' That is to say, martyrdom was the key ingredient in the spread of Christianity. The Pagans didn't have martyrs, really; in the Roman Empire, you performed religious duties with the same passion you put into going to the bathhouse, or buying your groceries. It was a civic function, something you did for appearances. Certainly nothing worth getting killed over.

"But martyrdom – this demonstration of incredible faith, this act of ultimate devotion – that was something amazing. Something that could win over the faith of a Pagan, to convince them to adopt the ways of this strange cult of Christ. What did they feel that drove them to such lengths, when the Roman religion couldn't move its followers at all?"

I took down notes haphazardly. Not so much for study purposes – Eccleston's classes were pretty easy to pass, as long as you turned in the homework – but so I could argue with him on the page. I knew what he meant by this little spiel: the Romans didn't care about their gods, so their religion wasn't really valid in the first place. Of course the pure faith of the Christians would let them take over.

But that was nonsense. I scribbled names down in the margins: *Eleusinians? Isis and Osiris? Mithras?* Can you point to a soldier bathing in the steaming blood of a sacrificial bull and not call that passionate? If so, I want to see how your dictionary defines the word.

"But martyrdom had its issues, of course." Like the bloody, unnecessary death, I'd assume. Eccleston continued. "Here's the big one: could every Christian be held to the standards of the martyr? How should they react to persecution?"

He learned on a wooden podium at the front of the class. *Relax. Don't you see how relaxed I am?* "Let's say you're a Christian. The year is 303. The Emperor Diocletian just started a big persecution of the church, because the Oracle at Didyma told him the Christians are interfering with Apollo's oracles and their ability to predict the future. There's stories passing through the community – you've heard one man was scourged with a whip, had salt and vinegar poured all over his body. Another was boiled alive. Still another had molten iron, white-hot, poured across his body until he died."

I shuddered, contemplating the sensation of that last one. I imagined the smell of blistering flesh and boiling fat and...

"And then the Emperor's men come knocking at your door." He looked down at the class roster on his podium, scanning through the names, and then looked up. He pointed at the middle of the class, at me. (No, I didn't end up in the back row doing crosswords. Give me a little credit.) "Louis? What would you do?"

"If my choices are between being boiled alive and lying about which god I liked best? I think I'd have to go with lying. I can't think of anything worth being tortured to death over."

"Sensible. Or at least it seems that way, doesn't it?" The professor nodded. "So you turn over your scriptures and you burn some incense to Jupiter and Romulus. All sins forgiven, right?"

"Right," I said.

"But remember, you're a Christian. Or you were. And in this period, the Christians were an insulated community, for the most part. Your family is probably Christian; your main associates almost certainly are. So you head back to the church after escaping your fate, and you find that none of your friends know what to do with you. What you did sounded reasonable – after all, you avoided execution and torture. Hard to blame you for that.

"But then somebody brings up the martyrs..."

Here we go.

"Because other people had been in your same position, Louis – asked to recant their beliefs, on pain of death. And they said, 'no, I won't betray my faith. I won't burn an offering to the false gods of Olympus.' And they were carted away, and they were murdered by the Empire. They stood up for their beliefs, and you did not. They must be better Christians than you, then. Mustn't they?" He cocked his head to the side. "Shouldn't you have laid down your life, as well?"

"But that's ludicrous," I said. "Did they really think Jesus would have been happier that his followers got scourged to death instead of burning a little incense for the other team? A dead Christian doesn't feed many hungry and doesn't clothe many poor."

"True enough... But the question caused one of the biggest schisms in the history of the church." He turned back to the chalkboard to jot some terms down. He wrote down the word 'traditore', and underlined it. "Constantine the Great – we'll get to him soon – Constantine the Great made Christianity legal, and threw the state behind it. When he did that, he reinstated a number of bishops who had turned over their texts to be burned. This caused quite a controversy; the Donatists called them *traditores*." He pointed to the board. "If that looks a lot like the word 'traitor', well, you have the idea.

"What the Donatists said was that they wanted a church of saints, not sinners. They said there should be no forgiveness for a *traditore* – that, in essence, you either picked martyrdom or damnation. No in-between. And they had a lot of support for that sentiment, an awful lot of support. The Donatists were still going in northern Africa for centuries after Rome fell."

Naturally, the church, that high bastion of redemption, would rather you died pointlessly, would have its bishops spend decades arguing against forgiveness. I should have figured. Even in matters of life and death – and pain, incredible pain – it came back to old men shouting their dogmas at each other. That is the history of Christian thought: martyrs, and old men, and the students forced to listen to them.

I looked around the room. The class was about an average size for Truman – 23, 24 students. Most have silver crosses around their necks, or wore t-shirts stating they'd graduated from Chapel Grove Methodist High or something like that. As you'd expect, this class attracted the Campus Crusade crowd. The rest of the class – including me, I guess – was filled with bored kids who wanted to get a degree in Philosophy and didn't understand why they had to sit through all of this Tertullian bullshit.

Dr. Eccleston talked for another twenty minutes, but I quit taking notes.

* * *

Grimey lost the coin flip that night, so he had to cook dinner. Thank God. I'd lost the flip the past three days and had begun to fear another streak like back in April, where I ended up cooking for three weeks without reprieve. But then, the streaks were part of the fun, too. We liked the randomness of the system – we were both attracted to a certain degree of willful irresponsibility.

That said, I'm not sure how big a victory it was. Sure, Grimey had to cook, but that meant I had no excuse for putting off Eccleston's homework.

I know I was going on about the generalities of the academic population earlier, but I don't want to paint them as generic or interchangeable; professors are all freaks in one way or another. Certain professors build up reputations for their idiosyncrasies, especially in Philosophy and Religion, where nobody expects them to seem reasonable in the first place. So they all start to develop reputations – this one medievalist philosopher got named the University's Grand Marshal, for instance, and started carrying her official club with her everywhere she went. She'd threaten to wallop you with it if you weren't taking a class seriously. This one medievalist took her job as the University's Grand Marshal very seriously. She carried her official club with her everywhere, threatened to wallop anybody who interfered with her students' education. Another guy, this white-haired German, had everyone get out of their seats and jump around the room, claimed an active body encouraged active thinking.

Eccleston wasn't as fun as those two, though. Mostly he was known for his homework: every reading came with a double-sided sheet of legal paper, full of questions and blank spaces. The first time I got one, I laughed – I could imagine needing all that space. Then I read the questions:

> *Describe the relationship between the Roman Empire and the Jewish race at the time of the birth of Christ. What provinces and cities were historically Jewish? Who were the local governors circa 30 A.D.? Describe the interactions between the following groups at the time of Christ: Sadducees, Pharisees, Sanhedrin.*

I would like to call your attention to the fact that at least six questions lurk in that morass.

All of the information lay in the textbooks, addressed in the order the worksheet posed the questions – usually I knew the gist of the answers just by reading subheadings. But a single item could tackle twenty pages of the main textbook, not to mention the four supplemental books he assigned the class.

Eccleston gave us about three inches to a question. Never in my life have I written so small.

"Jesus Christ," I said, cleaning the smeared ink from question #4 from my hand. "Why doesn't he just ask us to rewrite the goddamn chapter? It would be more honest."

"Who are you bitching about now?" asked Grimey. He looked up from the griddle, which was full of French toast. (Grimey makes breakfast-for-supper a lot when he loses the coin flip.)

"Eccleston. Christian Thought guy. I mean, these worksheets…"

"Oh, Dr. Eccleston?" I saw him flip a slice of toast, but it broke apart, and he dropped it on the floor. Grimey shuffled it off to the side with his toe. I'm not sure if we ever got around to cleaning it up. "I took Judaism with him, freshman year."

"I didn't know that." I gave Grimey a look-over, studying his facial features. Was Grimey Jewish? He'd never mentioned an interest in it before. "Why were you in Judaism?"

"Hadn't declared my major yet." Grimey eventually settled on English, after a failed semester in Physics. "Took it for my philosophy and religion elective." Ah. Well, that made sense. He looked over at the kitchen table. "Yep, same worksheets. Man, I remember one... Four lines of questions, and the last sentence was, I swear, *summarize the past six thousand years of the Jewish experience.*"

"What did you write?"

Grimey lifted the French toast with his spatula: three pieces for each of us, plus a couple of microwave sausage links and a slice of cantaloupe. "I just put down *Abraham, the Temple, persecutions, Nazis, Israel.* I mean, what else was there room for?" He brought the plates over and sat down; I did my share and got cans of soda from the fridge. We didn't use glasses. Most days we were doing good if we used the trash can.

"Did he take it?"

"He wrote *'you can do better than this'* in the margin, but yeah, he took it." He bit into a sausage link. "He's not a bad guy, really. I've had worse professors than old Doctor-Preacher."

"Heh. 'Doctor-Preacher?'" I took a gulp of soda. "Did your class call him that?"

"No. People from my church. 'Doctor-Preacher's trying to organize this year's Vacation Bible School and he...'"

"Wait, wait." I help up my fork, which impaled a piece of French toast. "What do you mean, *your* church?"

Grimey hesitated, tried to cover it up by taking a sip of his cola. "Uh, well, you know. Church. When my mom comes to visit. She makes me go to church."

"I thought your mom just took you to Pancake City on Sundays."

"Yeah. Pancake City." He chewed his bubblegum-pink lips

and cut up a piece of toast. "Pancake City and church."

"Your mom doesn't know you're Pagan?"

He sighed and set his silverware down. "Fuck no, my mom doesn't know. And she doesn't need to know. I mean, she's seen my room, she can probably take a guess. But I'm not bringing it up to her."

We ate in silence. For a minute the only thing to hear was the little clatter of knives and forks on dishwasher-safe plates.

"I guess it's a good thing your mom doesn't like me much, or I might have blurted something out," I said. "Sorry, man. I thought she knew."

"It's not a big deal," he said, but of course, that was a lie. I didn't press it any further.

"So... Eccleston is, what, a member?" I asked. "Some volunteer?"

"Dude, he's the pastor."

I sat down my fork. "What? He can't do that. He teaches at a state university."

"I don't think that matters. He does it in his free time. It's like a second job or something."

"How can he be objective about anything teaching religion if he's preaching on Sunday? Why would they trust a fucking Christian pastor to teach Judaism?"

Grimey shrugged and ate his French toast. "Tenure, I guess. It lets you go places."

* * *

White hot iron boiled inside of a slowly tipping cauldron. A stream of liquid metal began its descent from the lip of the container down to the leg below. The flesh – my flesh, I realized – cracked and peeled away, leaving hissing crevices for the molten iron to slip into. The pain was crippling – I prayed to go into shock, but it never came. Only more pain, piling on itself over and over, pain and the hideous light of heat, pain and the smell of my body burning away...

I woke to find myself in my own bed, covered in sweat. A dissociative moment followed. I couldn't tell whether I was in my bedroom in the Community Chest Apartments or whether I had been locked in a Byzantine dungeon, a legionnaire wearing trenches in my skin with a leather scourge.

I heard somebody crashing around in the kitchen. Grimey, probably – him or a really inept burglar. Grimey had gone out drinking, but I stayed in; I had work in the morning. My senses started to come back to me, and the revelry of Kirksville on a Friday night began to filter in through the window: the bacchanalia of undergraduate life, parading through the parking lots of this apartment complex and every one like it for a mile in any direction.

Alone among the drunken denizens of Kirksville, I had been dreaming of martyrdom.

The sensation of boiling iron finally subsided. Only the uncomfortable sweat now. I rubbed my temples and laid back down. I could still feel the adrenaline coursing through my system. I considered getting up for a beer to calm myself down. (Alcohol solves all problems, right?)

The distant thud of the Delta Chi party barn's bass echoed in the room. I took a deep breath and rolled over again.

Martyrs.

We're obsessed with martyrs. Jesus. St. Stephen. Hussain ibn Ali. Thomas Beckett. James Dean. Tupac...

It barely matters what they died for, whether they thought they were dying *for* something at all. We take their deaths and wrap ourselves into them, use them to make our own lives seem important and meaningful. There's something glamorous about a wrongful death... Something romantic.

I closed my eyes, preparing to venture back into the torture chambers.

We don't like happy endings, not really... Tragedy and failure are so much more fulfilling...

"I don't care about your fucking magic quarters." A man yelling in the kitchen. Not Grimey. *"Where's the goddamn scotch?"*

A mumbled reply, too low to hear, then, after a few rhythmless footsteps in the hallway, three hammer-blows to the hollow plastic door of my bedroom.

"Hey, Lou," Grimey said in a high, drunken warble. "Where did we put the scotch?"

I affected a waking groan. "We drank it all last week, Grimes."

"Damn it." A beat. "Oh, fuck. You were sleeping, were you, buddy?"

"No," I said with a sigh. Dumbfuck. "I wasn't sleeping at all."

* * *

Grimey looked like he was dressed for 3rd Grade Picture Day. I guess there was nothing specifically awkward about his suit and tie (dark blue, drizzled with periwinkles) – Grimey just wasn't built for suits. Grimey liked baggy jeans that jingled with the sound of silver chains and black t-shirts with snarky one-liners or the logos of metal bands. All his formalwear seemed laced with itching powder. The coat hung from his soft shoulders like a set of cheap drapes, and his pants were slightly longer than his legs, so he kept stepping on the bottom with the heels of his shoes. The shoes, I should note, were immaculately polished, but that just added to the caricature.

He looked out of the car window at the brick church on the Square and gave me a look of delicious annoyance. "I can't fucking believe we're doing this. That you're making me do this."

"Calm down," I said. "They know you here, don't they?"

"That's my point!" said Grimey.

I had brought the idea up to him the night before, after I'd gotten home from work. I was cooking (I'd lost the flip) and told him I wanted to see one of Eccleston's sermons. He hated the idea from the outset. "They're going to ask me about my mom and why I haven't been coming to services and whether I'm going to volunteer to, I don't know, paint the rec center or something. It's embarrassing." I only convinced him to go with me after I promised to vacuum the apartment. (This is a bigger deal than it sounds, since it involved plumbing the depths of the closet to find out where we had stuck the vacuum after the last time we'd cleaned, approximately three days after we moved in.)

I looked around for somewhere to park. "It's really not such a big deal."

"Obviously it is, or we wouldn't have come in the first place." He sighed. "Don't make it seem like I'm being unreasonable. You're the obsessive one here."

We parked across the street. I couldn't see any indication of which door to go through; the church seemed more like a walled compound. It had four visible white doors and the potential for more hidden in alleys and rear walls. None of them looked ostentatious enough to be the entrance.

"How the hell do we get in?" I asked.

"You parked on the wrong side of the building, dumbass," said Grimey. "Come on."

Grimey led me to the other side, where an ornate door flanked by pale Grecian columns waited. A young woman in a blue dress and a young man wearing a white shirt but no coat stood at the doors with leaflets. Neither of them acknowledged Grimey. I think Grimey was relieved not to be recognized.

I took a lime-green flier and read it over:

September 16, 2006
Corpus Christi Baptist Church
David Eccleston, Pastor

'To teach the word of the Lord, to follow His commands,
To share His gospel, to glorify His name'

Church news followed. Choir practice had been canceled. Deacon Lindquist would be absent next week to attend a conference in Boise. The Youth Service Corps needed money to go to New Orleans to help renovate houses after Hurricane Katrina. I crumpled the flier into a pocket and we went in.

I had no idea how *red* this church would be until Grimey and I were inside. All the pews were covered in crimson upholstery, and the walls were the color of a thin scab. The scarlet carpet squished a half inch with every step; I felt like I was wading through a coagulated river. The aisle led to a series of wide stairs with a podium at the top. At least that was wood-grained. Plants waited in pots behind the podium, but the sanguine tint of the room made even the most innocent fern look sinister.

"I thought churches were supposed to be all white and pure," I whispered to Grimey.

"Maybe it's to let us know where we're headed."

We sat down in a pew near the middle. Middle-aged women in conservative dresses had us flanked on all sides. I looked around the room and soaked in the scenery: the pillars that held up the balcony and the ceiling, the brass crosses that dominated the walls, the tall and narrow windows that dispersed the sunlight into diffracted radiance.

Grimey reached for the hymnal and tried to bury himself in it, but within thirty seconds the woman to his left looked at him and gasped.

"Herman! I haven't seen you here in weeks."

If Grimey looked at me, he would have seen my face bent around one word: *Herman?* But he didn't. He sounded like a mall guard on Black Friday. "Hi, Mrs. Beaumont."

"It's so good to see you," she said. "How are you? How is your mother?"

"We're both fine," said Grimey. *Herman?* Grimey.

Mrs. Beaumont patted him on the shoulder. "You haven't been here – busy with school, I suppose – so you might not have heard, but big things are happening around here. Some of the boys are repainting the gymnasium, and if you have the time..."

* * *

The Sweater Prof was a Suit Preacher: dark gray coat, crisp white shirt, violet tie. In the classroom, a suit implies formality, distance, says *stay at arm's length*. It's different at the pulpit. There it means something else: *I'm a man of God, but I'm a man, just the same. I'm not some mystic, some priest in a long black robe. I'm a preacher, but the Man Upstairs talks to all of us. I'm one of you – just the one up front.* The same message as the sweater, really. Context is everything.

He opened with a Bible verse – Mark something something – and a brief prayer. It seemed pretty standard – "traditional" – but I admit that I have no idea what that means. I've only been in Christian churches a handful of times in my life. I had been to a Catholic service once with my grandmother, before she died; that had been much more reserved and formal than this. But a friend I'd made in a Plato study group had convinced me to go with him to another Baptist Church here in Kirksville last year, and the preacher there had pulled out a Telecaster and started playing Christian rock.

Churches don't seem to have any cohesion to me. They talk as though they all worship the same God, but that God seems to have very different priorities depending on where you spent your Sundays. He needed some people to stand up and kneel down in the right order, and he needed some people to sing the hymns to the beat of a five-piece drum kit, and he didn't need anything from some people at all, because their salvation had been determined before the world began.

But despite the differences, they had one thing in common: they were the True Faith. The details mattered, of course; they argued about them, and sometimes, they murdered each over them. But one of the churches, somewhere, had it exactly right. History was a process of refining religion into its true form, from the barbaric totems of primitive man through the hedonistic gods of the Pagans to the One True God, who, by definition, was all perfection, all beauty, all benevolence. Anything that did not point to that god was backward-looking heresy.

I'd never believed in any of that. My parents had turned away from the churches of their parents while they were in their 20s, and they'd brought me up in their new religion, as a child of Witches. They'd inculcated me with their worldview: of the goodness of the Earth, of the falsehood of sin, of the infuriating bullshit the Christians called theology.

And yet... And yet.

Part of me always wonders if they are right.

And in the pit of that doubtful fragment of my soul, a sliver of my heart knows they are, and will never believe anything else.

Not cell, not an atom, of my being could be called Christian. But there are days I know I am going to Hell.

"Friends, I want to talk to you about something today," Pastor Eccleston said, beginning his... Sermon? Homily? I forget the terminology. "Something called apostasy. It's a word we don't use much anymore, but we should. It comes from the Greek, meaning 'standing apart'. It's a word we use for people who have turned their backs on God, who have decided to stand apart from Him and His word."

The pastor leaned on his pulpit, just as he leaned on his podium in the classroom. "I've got a story to tell you about a young man I knew back in seminary. This young man..." He paused to think. "He was a handsome fellow. Broad shoulders. Good teeth. And everybody said he was smart, and a good worker. His parents had been quite proud of him, of all he'd accomplished by the time he was in seminary.

"This young man had known from the time he was six years old that he wanted to be a pastor, as his father had been, as his grandfather had been. So he worked hard in school and he got accepted into a fine seminary. I might be biased, of course, since I *am*, of course, speaking about my own seminary."

Grimey looked like his eyes had been stapled open. The middle-aged women, however, seemed rapt. Admittedly, Eccleston had a fine voice for the pulpit: a steady baritone with just a hint of folksy wheeze. Sort of like Garrison Keillor.

"So he goes to seminary and studies. But you know, in seminary, you spend a lot of time looking over the scripture and reading scholarship... Things come up, things you never expected to find. You read about the different dates people attribute to the gospels. Different translations of the Greek. Sometimes you run across something that contradicts everything you'd been taught – that although your copy of the bible has the word 'Lord' everywhere, there's really all kinds of different words that the translators put in as 'Lord'. They just never bothered to tell you there was any difference between them.

"So this young man starts to question things. He thinks to himself, 'This is all so inconsistent. What happened to my eternal truth? What happened to my Word of God?' Eventually, he starts to think that it's all a big mistake, a joke with no punchline. And he quits the seminary. And he quits the church. He turns his back on God. He becomes an apostate. It happens all the time.

"You all are smart people. You might have guessed who that young man really was, I'm thinking. It was, of course, me."

He paused to take a drink of water. Nobody made a sound, not even an unruly child.

"I quit seminary about a year before I would have finished, moved up to Chicago and taught Introduction to Religious Studies at a community college. I didn't have anything to do with the church – really, nothing to do with God. I wasn't quite an atheist, but I wouldn't have called myself a Christian. I regarded it all as superstition. Things just didn't add up.

"I went home for Christmas one year – I guess I was about thirty – and my mother insisted that I go to my father's Christmas service. I went just to placate her, the way so many young people do.

"But I got to the church that morning, and saw my father, this 67-year-old man, up at that pulpit. He was just preaching his heart out. He was one of your old-style preachers, all passion and fire and vigor – not so cautious as his son turned out to be." He smiled, gently. "At first I looked at him and I thought how silly he sounded. He said a line from Matthew that I remembered from a class I took. We had looked at eight different translations of that verse. Every one of them seemed like a completely different sentence. None of them seemed to match up with the rest. I remember that.

"But then..." Eccleston paused, took a deep, speech-turning breath. "But you know, I heard the fire in my father's voice. I heard the Holy Spirit behind him. At that point in his life, he was already having troubles: heart problems, hip problems, bad arthritis. But up there, on that pulpit, he moved like a man thirty years younger, like a man who'd had his burden lifted. It was beautiful. I saw him in a way I never had before, that day.

"Friends, I went home after that service and poked around at the old family bible. I re-read some of the finest parts of scripture: John 3, Corinthians, the Sermon on the Mount. And you know what? I realized that I had been looking at the wrong thing, the whole time. I had been looking at these quibbles that didn't really matter. Sure, the Bible has its flaws – flaws introduced by men who were imperfect, as I was imperfect. But God was there. He was there in my father's breast that Christmas morning, and He was there, in the words of scripture. And He is here, right now, in each of us. You can get lost in details. You can miss the forest for the trees."

He stood up to his full height and looked down at us, his smile reserved and kind. "It's not our place, friends, to judge those who have turned from the path, who have been seduced by the traps and conundrums that surround us. People get lost in the details, and they have to work their way out of that thicket in their own way, with the help of the Lord. It's not our place to hunt the apostates among us, who might be among us in this very church, today. Sometimes it takes time for people to come around." He closed his book. "Sometimes it just takes time."

He finished with a prayer. Everyone bowed their heads but Grimey and I, and one young man two rows ahead of us. Grimey and I looked at each other. I don't know what he read in my face.

Grimey put in a dollar when they passed around the till, but I passed the plate to the woman on my right with nothing more added than the warmth of my hand.

* * *

Grimey managed to escape without being pressed into painting anything. He got in the car and slammed the door. "Well, I'm sure glad we did that this morning instead of sleeping in." He groused and put on his seatbelt. "Can't think of anything I would have rather done."

"I thought it was enlightening," I said.

"Huh?"

"Just listen to the bullshit people will eat if you know how to present it. I mean, what was the moral of that story? 'Facts don't matter! Everything about Christianity disproves itself and all the dogma is a fabrication, but, gosh darn it, daddy knew how to preach, and that proves God is real!' Really? Just fuck me."

I started the engine and pulled out. Grimey leaned back and rested his elbow on the door. "I don't know, man. I mean, at least he said it's not anybody's place to judge, right? He's talking about how you should be nice to people, even if they aren't in the church. That's better than fire and brimstone."

"He said it's nobody's place to judge because eventually all the heretics will realize their mistakes and give in to the One True Way. It's bullshit."

"I think you're taking this too seriously, Lou."

We passed through the Square and headed down Franklin Street toward the Community Chest.

"Yeah, well, I don't think you take it seriously enough."

We got back to the apartment without speaking any more. Grimey went into his room to change into something black and spiky.

I went into my room and slipped off my shoes, threw the dirty socks into the sedimentary layers of laundry on my floor. I continued running through the contours of the Preaching Professor's sermon. (Sermon. It's got to be a sermon.) About heretics, and apostates, and the One True Way.

The inevitable, inescapable, One True Way.

That's logic, isn't it? Somewhere there's a correct answer, and when you find it, everything else is proven wrong. Who knows how you would act when you found that kind of truth? Would you spend your whole life telling everyone else about it? Would you run off and become a hermit, content to live in the beatific peace of true knowledge?

Would you die for it?

I sat there staring at the altar of my gods of reason. They stared back, unblinking. It felt like the statues were judging me, solving me like an algebraic equation.

I walked over to the altar. I picked up a handkerchief from the floor, the cleanest thing in arm's reach. I started to angrily dust off the statues of my gods, and just as angrily, I started to pray.

III

The voice, boisterous and blasphemous and full of warmth, grabbed me from the arms of sleep and dragged me into the waking world.

And anyone who had heart, he wouldn't turn around and break it!

And anyone who played a part, he couldn't turn around and hate it, no, no, no!

"Not sweet Jane," I mumbled in unison with Lou Reed. I shuddered and looked at the clock: 3:57 PM. Shit. It had only been four hours since Grimey and I had gotten home from church. I had work later on in the evening and needed the sleep. I considered ignoring the call and rolling over, but I grudgingly rolled over and picked up my phone. The pixilated face of a girl with turquoise hair smiled at me from the screen.

"Hey, Lucy," I said, trying to keep the phlegm from my voice.

"Hey you," she said. "Busy?"

"Not especially," I said. I sat up, back against the wall, and stifled a yawn. "What's up?"

"Did I wake you up?" Lucy asked. "It's like, five."

"I didn't get home until noon."

"Oh." She paused. "I'm sorry. Do you want me to call back later? I didn't mean to wake you."

"No, no, it's fine."

"Well, alright..." She demurred for a moment, then continued. "I wanted to ask you a favor. Are you going home this weekend?"

I ran over some dates. Today was the 16th, so then... Friday would be the 21st. "Shit. I forgot all about Harvest Home. I hadn't really made plans, but I guess I should."

"Actually, it's good if you aren't," she said. "Well, good for me, anyway. I got a paper into a conference this weekend, down at Mizzou."

"Congratulations." I meant it, but in my sleepy haze, it might have sounded sarcastic.

"Thanks," she said. "I don't really know anyone in Columbia, and it's a pretty long drive from here, so I was wondering if I could crash at your apartment over the weekend."

"Sure, of course. Mi casa es su casa." I could feel the saltwater finally draining out of my mind. A mixed blessing – it would be that much harder to fall asleep again. "Why aren't you just going to St. Louis?"

"Well, I would if I were going to *your* parents' house, Lou. But the farm is fifty miles south of I-70. It would tack on an hour each way." Lucy's parents lived on this little farm they called 'the Elysian Fields', about forty minutes south of St. Louis. Well, forty minutes the way I drive. "Plus I got into this big argument with my mom last week, and I don't really want to have to go through round two the night before I give a big paper."

"I know the feeling," I said. "Sure, it'll be fun. I'll try to get off of work."

"Awesome. Thank you so much." I heard a discordant note in her dreamy voice; anxiety, maybe? Hell, I don't know. It was probably just me. The whole world looks anxious on four hours of sleep.

"Maybe we can do something for Harvest Home while you're here?"

"Sure, that would be great," she said. "Listen, I better let you get back to sleep, huh? You sound pretty beat."

"More sleep wouldn't be the worst thing that ever happened to me."

"Oh yeah?" For the first time in the conversation, I could hear her smile into the receiver. "What was the worst thing, then?"

"I met you. That was pretty bad."

"So the worst moment of your life happened when you were six months old?"

"That seventh month was killer."

I could *hear* that girl roll her eyes. "Get some sleep, Lou."

"I will. See you this weekend, Valkyrie."

Lucy hung up, and I set the phone back on my bed stand. (By "bed stand," I mean "three mismatched plastic bins with a lamp and clock on top.")

I laid in bed for an hour or so and couldn't get back to sleep. Eventually I got up, put on pants, and pulled out my homework. I was finished with Logic for the week, and caught up with my other classes, so I turned to Eccleston's class. I hadn't looked at the worksheet yet, and I trembled in horrid expectation.

We had a break from the arguing bishops that week. The readings were all about the House of Constantine – the emperors who made Rome a Christian empire. Everybody knows about Constantine, I hope – he was the emperor who saw, or at least claimed he saw, after the fact, the sign of Christ in the sky over the Milvian Bridge prior to a major battle. "By this sign, conquer." (Not, "By this sign, feed the hungry," nor "By this sign, bring peace." "By this sign, conquer.") He won the battle. And after that, there wasn't much question about which religion was on the rise in the Roman Empire. He defunded the Pagan temples and made the bishops play nice at Nicea. He never converted openly, not until he was on his deathbed, at any rate. But he was the first Christian emperor, the first to realize how much easier it would be to control a world when everyone was made to worship the same god.

His sons, Constans, and Constantius, and Constantine II – you may detect a certain theme in the naming – were all murderous bastards, but they kept up their support of the church. They even picked their favorite heresies to side with, I presume to justify more paranoid murders. They never made Christianity the official religion – that didn't happen until Theodosius, a few decades later – but they didn't have to. For forty years, the church was the favored institution of the Augustus. And enough Romans – hardly all, but enough – knew which way that wind would blow.

Forty years, and the grand religion of Olympus, which stretched back into the darkness of history, had nearly crumbled to ashes.

But then there was Julian.

He was born a prince, unfortunately, and because he was a prince he was the enemy of the emperor Constantius. The emperor murdered Julian's entire family while Julian was a baby. Only two survived. One was Julian's brother, Gallus, who was a cripple and expected to die; the other was Julian, who, as a baby, presumably had not yet learned the skills needed to overthrow an emperor.

Constantius had a problem, however. He needed a Caesar – a figure to represent imperial power, a vice emperor, if you will. And he had systematically eliminated every member of his family except for the two boys. He made Gallus Caesar, but Gallus turned out to be a brute and a madman. Constantius had him murdered too. ("Thou shalt not kill" is the most important commandment.)

When Julian was in his 20s, Constantius realized that he needed someone to put down a rebellion in Gaul while he governed in the east. He also realized he had murdered every reasonable candidate for the job except for Julian – Julian, who was just a dreaming scholar at this point, spending every moment reading books and visiting philosophers. Julian received a summons from the emperor and was crowned Caesar by the man who had killed his entire family and forced him to live his youth in exile.

Nobody expected much of Julian; he was supposed to sit back as a figurehead, be an imperial face at the back of the army. But he did good. He was a hell of a general. Granted, he really just followed Julius Caesar's playbook when he invaded Gaul, but Julius wrote a pretty good playbook.

He did other things, too – he slept in the barracks with his men, he did their workouts, he refused any luxury that would have been denied to them. His men grew to love him – and the Roman army always eventually did one thing to a leader they loved. One night Julian found himself proclaimed Augustus. Emperor. Constantius had murdered every one of his relatives to prevent the rise of a rival Augustus, and Julian, the last one alive, had done it anyway. It was like something out of *Highlander*. Or, more appropriately, from a Greek tragedy – like Laius and Oedipus. In attempting to thwart destiny, he fulfilled it.

Julian and his army made their way to Constantinople to face Constantius; civil war seemed inevitable. But then a strange sort of miracle happened: Constantius caught a fever. He died en route to Constantinople, and in a moment of humility, sent word ahead that Julian was to be received as the sole legitimate Augustus. Julian entered the capital city that summer as sole ruler of the greatest empire known to humanity.

And at that moment, he threw away a lifetime of pretense and falsehood, and showed the world that he was no follower of Christ. A Pagan emperor reigned again. The rule of the gods of old had been restored.

I think a lot about Julian in that moment. What it must have felt like, to finally reveal his true self to the world. He had been Pagan for years by that point – perhaps, in his heart, for his whole life. And yet nobody knew, except a handful of teachers and confidants. He would have been killed immediately if the emperor had found out. Even as Caesar – nominally the second most powerful man in the world – he had been forced to keep the secret.

So then how did it feel to at last be free of that mask? It is impossible to know. But I hope – I pray – that it was glorious, a moment of perfection that stood out against a lifetime of pain and paranoia, a moment of pure joy. The gods lived. My gods – the gods who stand on my altar, right now, today – lived again in the streets of Rome.

And then the stupid fucker got himself killed trying to be

Alexander the Great.

I read in one of Eccleston's books that when Julian died, the Christian bishops cheered. "The little cloud has passed," they said. "The little cloud." Rome passed back into the hands of the Christians, and so did we all.

They called Constantine "the Great" because he converted the empire to Christ, breaking with thousands of years of tradition. For trying to restore the faith Rome had been built on, breaking with the rule of only a few decades, Julian received an epithet of his own. For the next 1500 years, whenever some partisan of the church needed to invoke a villain, they needed only mention the name of the hated *traditore*, the false emperor, Julian the Apostate.

* * *

Eccleston was late to his office hours on Tuesday, which I found infuriating. What the hell was the point of posting the hours on your door if you couldn't be bothered to follow them? 11:00 AM to 1:00 PM, Tuesday and Thursday. It was 11:15 already.

I was naturally annoyed that I needed to speak with Eccleston in the first place – the veneer of folksy charm was more overpowering one-on-one than in a group setting. I also had Logic in forty-five minutes, and for whatever reason, they stuck that class over in Violette Hall, the math building. (Well, okay, I guess Logic is kind of mathematical, but – look, holding a Philosophy class halfway across the campus from the Philosophy department is just a dumb idea.)

I sank down into the horrifying orange couches in the hallway outside the Philosophy and Religion offices. I have friends in Truman's Design program, but I don't trust them – not while McClain Hall still exists. From the outside it looks okay: just a generic brick building with big glass doors. From the inside, though... Jesus Christ. Who made the decision to base the décor around beige walls, orange couches, and purple carpeting? It's like they were picked out of an acid flashback. Down here in the back halls, the effect is compounding with dim Noir lighting. Sometimes you're apt to think Phillip Marlowe could come walking through the halls, pausing to comment on the garish scenery before kicking in a professor's door.

I needed to talk to Eccleston about my term paper. Most people were writing about some St. Ignatius bullshit, and the thought of that made me want to trade places with Sisyphus. I knew exactly what I wanted to write about, of course – but the game rules said I needed his approval first.

At last I heard the jingling march of a man holding a full ring of keys approaching down the hallway. 11:21. Slacker. Dr. Eccleston appeared, holding a stack of essays in one hand and his keys in the other; he wore a brown sweater-vest with a lavender undershirt. The sweater-vest was the kind you'd be embarrassed to get from your aunt at Christmas. He smiled when he saw me, clearly caught off guard that anyone actually visited him during office hours. "Ah, hello, Louis. Are you here to see me?"

"Yes, sir," I said. *Sir.* What a puss.

"Just give me a second to get in the door..." He struggled with his papers, and then gestured to me with the stack. "Could you give me a hand with these?"

I took his papers. First essays for another one of his classes: Exploring Religions, the 101 course. I saw that the top paper was about Hinduism. How could he teach this in good faith? What could a man like him have to say about Shiva?

He opened the door. Eccleston kept an orderly office: alphabetical bookshelves, no clutter, an in-box and out-box next to his computer. It's always hard to know what to expect about professors' offices; just next door to his, one professor (the Grand Marshal – you know, the one with the club?) has an office that is completely, every single inch, covered in journals and books and articles and gods know what else. She acknowledges that you will inevitably step on something irreplaceable trying to get to a chair, but she just shrugs, says she can read around the footprints.

"Thanks, Lou," said Dr. Eccleston. He took the papers back, shuffled them into a perfectly rectangular pile, and stacked them in the in-box. He sat down in his chair – a plush black office chair, quite different from the orange plastic chair I had. "So what can I help you with?"

"I wanted to talk to you about my term paper," I said. "I know it's pretty early in the semester, but I wanted to get a head start."

"Starting early is a sign of a determined thinker," he said. "What's on your mind?"

"Well... I know he isn't technically a Christian thinker, but considering how important he was to the period, I'd like to write about Julian the Apostate."

Saying the name out loud like that filled me with a strange disgust; my tongue shriveled under the syllables. *Apostate.* They should have called him Julian the Philosopher. He had shaped himself in the mold of Marcus Aurelius, after all; he would have preferred a life of thoughtful debate in Athens to a life at court in Constantinople. But people respect philosophers. (Or they did in the ancient world, anyway.) But an apostate? You can cheer the man who stabs an apostate to death as a saint.

Still, the name had never revoked that reaction in me before. I didn't know what to think about it. I stammered on. "I – I was rather taken with the chapter we read last week."

Dr. Eccleston leaned back in his chair and tapped his fingers against his chin like an old Taoist sage. "Hmm. Well, there's no denying his importance – he defined the entire course of the church, for a few years, anyway. And few people in the period are more interesting in their own right. A romantic hero and all that." He nodded his head back and forth. "What would you be writing about, specifically? The course is about Christianity, after all... What's your connection?"

"The way he approached Pagan charity was really interesting to me," I said. "That whole idea that Christianity only won so many converts because the Christians let the poor eat for free. He wasn't single-minded about reinstating Paganism – he wanted to reform it, you know? He wasn't above taking inspiration from the Christians when they did something right."

"Indeed." He turned on an electric coffee pot that sat next to his computer. "I'm always fascinated by how much this supposed 'apostate' borrowed directly from Christian morality. Many people have written about how Christian Julian remained in his heart – he just expressed it with different metaphors."

I huffed. "Different metaphors? That seems like a stretch to me. I mean, he endorsed a totally different religion. The whole marketplace of divinity..."

"Julian's fundamental policy was to impose Christian hierarchy upon the Olympian pantheon, when we boil it down." He said that forcefully, shutting me down. He looked at his shelf and pulled down a book. "Here... Give this one a read. You might find it useful."

I looked it over: a painting – it looked to be late Renaissance, maybe, certainly far later than Roman art – of a blond-haired youth. It was simply titled *The Last Pagan*. Endorsements from *The Catholic Herald* and *The Church Times* spread across the back cover.

I took it without complaint. No point. "Thanks, professor."

"Not a problem, Lou. Come back when you've got a draft started and we'll see what we can come up with, okay?"

I nodded and started to stand up, but I got this odd compulsion as I did, and sat back down. "Hey, Dr. Eccleston. Can I ask another question?"

"These *are* my office hours," he said. "That's what I'm here for."

"Well, it's another thing about Julian. Just... Purely hypothetical."

He smiled his kindly-uncle smile. I wondered how much he was acting. "Shoot," he said.

"What do you think would have happened if Julian hadn't gone on campaign? What if he'd just gone to Constantinople – lived to be an old man?"

He shrugged. "I'm not sure I see the point of the question. It's a matter of historical fact. He died; his plans failed with him. They were already failing when he was killed, truth be told."

"I know it's historical fact. Still. What if he'd lived?"

"Do you mean, would Europe have gone back to Paganism?" He considered this for a moment, and then shrugged. "No, I doubt it. The forces of Christianization were already too entrenched at that point. Julian's cause was always a lost one. Romantic, but deeply impractical."

I hesitated before pressing it any further. "Do you think it was a good thing, then, that he died when he did?"

His smile broadened, but it was a chimpanzee grin, full of quiet frustration and dominance. "Lou, again, it's a matter of history. Whether it's a good thing or a bad thing is irrelevant; it happened."

"I know, but... Still. Are you glad it turned out the way it did?"

He sighed, ran his fingers through his thin hair. "Well, if he hadn't, I'm not sure I would be here – certainly not having this conversation with you. Even though I think he would have failed in the end, there are a lot of things that I take for granted in my life that might not exist if he had been around longer. Julian lived long enough to end many of the church's schisms, but not long enough to ruin the church as a whole as he'd wanted to. If he had... Well, who could say what things would be like now?" He sat up and looked at me again. "So while I dislike the idea of anybody dying violently in the first place, least of all a man who tried to be noble and ethical... I suppose, if pressed, I am glad it turned out as it did. As I said, we wouldn't be here if it hadn't."

I guess that was a fair enough answer – honest, even if he still tried to weasel out of it with all that "whatever happened, happened" talk. I got up, took his book, and shook Dr. Eccleston's hand. "Thanks, Professor. I was just curious."

"It's a good trait in a philosopher," he said. "Have a nice afternoon, Louis."

I walked out through the cavernous hallways of McClain Hall and back into the sunlight. My encounter with Eccleston had only taken a few minutes – I had enough time before Logic that I could stroll along the brick byways of the Truman State campus. I took in the last breaths of summer; the whispers of fall could only barely be heard in the cooling wind. The quadrangle was green and lush, full of Frisbee players and freshman couples huddling on blankets.

I watched those people on the quad as I walked. They reminded me of when I was a kid, when I used to visit Andy and Lucy at the Elysian Fields over the summer. The four of us... Andy and Lucy and Lou and Dottie, playing tag in the fields, swimming in the duck pond, building bonfires behind the house. I would spend whole months there, sleeping on the floor in Andy's room, where we planned daring midnight raids into the girls' room. I can't remember any time when I was happier than those summers with Dottie and the Walsteads.

Sometimes I wonder why they stopped: why I never stayed with them anymore once I turned 14, why we grew apart like we did. And then other times I remember them in their perfect eternity. I see them in Lucy's face, which still shines like eternal summer.

I ran my fingers across the spine of the paperback book, looking it over again. A history of the rise and fall of Julian the Apostate. *The Last Pagan.*

But he wasn't, was he?

* * *

Lucy's car, a white Chevrolet Cavalier, pulled up outside the Community Chest around 7:30 on Friday night. She had dyed her hair again: she'd gone back to blue, but more of a royal blue than the turquoise she used to wear. I watched as she jumped out of her car and grabbed a pearl-colored suitcase from the back seat.

"Hey you!" I called from my window.

"Hey yourself!" She grinned up at me and bounded toward the door.

I went downstairs to let her in. I offered to take her suitcase, but she wouldn't let me. Grimey looked up from the TV when we got back to the apartment and gave her a silent greeting with a wave of his hand. Then he turned his attentions back to the set.

I had voluntarily thrown the coin flip that night. (Over Grimey's protests, I might add – he complained that I was screwing up some perfectly good chaos.) I wanted to cook for Lucy, because I'm a sap. All cynics are romantics at heart.

The first time I had a serious girlfriend, freshman year of college, I'd called my dad a few days before Valentine's Day to ask him what I could cook to impress a girl. He said he always preferred lobster, but given my general state of (and I quote my father directly here) "broke-assedness," a good Quiche Lorraine would do the trick. Turned out to be a bad choice: that girl was lactose intolerant.

And I know what you're thinking. "How did you not know that beforehand?" And the answer is... Well, maybe I wasn't such a good boyfriend. I just didn't know. We got Chinese and I ate quiche for a week.

Anyway, regardless of that first incident, I've still held out faith in the old man's advice, so... I made Lucy a quiche.

She took it with a bemused smile. "Since when did you learn how to cook, Lou?"

Grimey looked positively disturbed. "Seriously. I was expecting Mystery Mac'n'Cheese."

"It's Harvest Home! You're supposed to feast." I poured us all glasses from the wine jug. "So shut up and feast."

We dug in, ate, drank cheap wine. Grimey and I listened to Lucy tell us about the paper she'd be presenting tomorrow afternoon. We pretended to understand; it had something to do with derivational syntax, whatever that was. She was way over my head.

This was a disadvantage I'd had with Lucy for years. I mean, anyone who reads books can bullshit philosophy well enough. I knew the details, but she knew enough of the basics to keep up with me. And she was probably better-versed in a lot of the comparative religions – I never could get into Eastern religion, but her parents always had a soft spot for the Buddhists.

Meanwhile, she was a linguist, and I had no clue about that. I remember once when she called me at two in the morning, positively giggling over learning Korean. Her voice had the same ecstatic lilt of pothead discussing Pink Floyd. "You just don't understand it, Lou. This agglutinative construction stuff is so fucking cool."

"You're right," I said. "I don't understand it."

Grimey didn't talk much throughout dinner. I didn't understand why at the time. Grimey was pretty outgoing – more outgoing than he really had the talent for, honestly – but he seemed distracted that night. But, you know. We were young men, and better friends than we would ever admit to each other. You men have unspoken laws. One of the first Guy Laws I learned was not to pry too deeply into your buddy's mind without being asked – and sometimes, even if you *are* asked – so I didn't press him about it.

When she was finished with her quiche, Lucy raised a toast. "Happy Mabon. It's good to spend it with family."

Family? Ouch. I wasn't sure how I felt about that, even though no other word could really describe my relationship with Lucy.

Grimey and I raised our glasses – his a pint glass, mine a

bourbon snifter – and clinked them together. Then we drained the last of the sour wine.

"What time do you need to be up tomorrow, Luce?" I asked, once the obligatory post-feast yawning and stretching had finished.

"Pretty early – I think I need to make it to Columbia by nine AM or so. Maybe a little later if I'm willing to miss the first session." She leaned forward onto her elbows, rested her chin in her hands. "Why, what did you have in mind?"

"Well... It *is* Harvest," I said. "I mean, since neither of us is going to make it home for the ritual tomorrow... I thought maybe we could do something. Nothing fancy, you know, but something. Maybe go out to Thousand Hills, the state park?"

"I didn't bring any of my ritual stuff, but... Sure, that sounds fun." She turned to Grimey, who jumped out of his post-supper trance when he realized she was talking to him. "You want to come, Grimey?"

Well, fuck. Why did she do that?

"Uh. Sure. Sounds great – just let me get my jacket."

Grimey went to his bedroom to get his coat. I started to clean up – a lengthy process that consisted of grabbing the dirty dishes and dumping them into the sink to age to perfection.

"Oh, I forget to tell you on the phone earlier," I said while turning on the tap for our patented 'cold-water soak' method. "I tried, but I couldn't convince them to let me off tonight. I've got to go in around midnight."

"That stinks," Lucy said. She scratched something out on her essay, then bit her lip and erased the scratches. "Well... Maybe I can keep you company for a little while? I mean, I need to get *some* sleep before tomorrow, but..."

"That's completely against company policy down at Cheriton." I dumped the last of the dishes into the sink. "Notice how I said that like I give a fuck."

IV

By the time we drove the handful of miles north of town to Thousand Hills, the sun had already set. I think, technically, this meant we were trespassing, but people did it all time. The park rangers generally bought the excuse of ignorance and let you go without a ticket.

They built the park back in the 50s, I think. They dammed up the creek to make Kirksville's water supply. (In all fairness, it resulted in a very pretty lake.) I didn't make it out there nearly as often as I should have. The last time I'd been there was probably the year before, when I barbecued at the lake with Grimey and a handful of other people. Grimey had a stand-off with a raccoon that day that remains legendary among our cohort; it was a miracle he didn't get rabies.

We pulled off the road by the lake shelters. The gate had been closed off for the night, so we had to walk down to the shore. The full moon hung low and the light of Mother Luna made the stars seem like tiny pricks in a pane of frosted glass.

I had packed a small box of ritual supplies and thrown it in the trunk. It wasn't much – an athame (a gift from Lucy's parents after my initiation), two bowls (one for salt, one for water), a chalice (easily the nicest drinking vessel I owned), a sword (a beat-up replica Civil War saber), some incense (not Nag Champa, thank gods), three candles (white, black, and red), and the wine and cakes (Three Buck Chuck and a box of Famous Amos.) Not much, but enough for a makeshift altar on the shore of the lake.

"I didn't bring a robe," said Lucy as she helped me set up the altar. "Guess that means I'll have to go skyclad, huh?" If only.

Lucy still looked the part better than either of us. We wore jeans and hoodies; at least Lucy had a skirt, one of those long, flowing brown ones with embroidery on the hem. She slipped her shoes off and wiggled her toes in the cool grass. She did the same thing the first time I ever visited the Elysian Fields: Lughnasadh, when we were kids...

"Probably for the best that we don't have robes," said Grimey. "This is gonna look weird enough if a ranger comes by and catches us."

"Catches us? Catches us doing what?" Lucy asked. "I don't think it's against the law to burn a candle. I mean, unless we're stupid about it."

"I meant, well..." Grimey swallowed. "Just that the ritual might look weird, to some cowen."

"Don't worry about it," said Lucy. "Just relax – we'll be fine."

"You want to do the quarters, Grimey?" I asked. "There's only three of us, we'll have to jury-rig some things."

"Uh, sure," he said. "When do I do those...?"

"Right after Lucy finishes casting the circle," I said. "It's easy."

We joined hands there, in front of the lake and the starry night, taking deep breaths. I felt the warmth from both of their hands – supple heat from Lucy's long fingers, the clamminess of Grimey's palm. I closed my eyes and tried to focus on clearing my mind of all things but two. Perfect love and perfect trust. Bring nothing with you but perfect love and perfect trust.

I knelt down and drew a pentagram into the bowl of salt. Lucy took the sword and walked around us, drawing a circle in the air. "This is the circle," she said. "This is the space between the worlds. Here be magick. Here be love. So mote it be."

"So mote it be," I said. Grimey started to get the idea.

I mixed the salt and water and drew a spiral emanating outward – widdershins or counter-widdershins, I could never remember which was which – and handed it to Lucy.

"May this circle be as a still and silent pool, its love radiating outward in ever-widening circles," she said, her voice like a waking dream. "So mote it be."

"So mote it be," we said in unison.

Finally I lit the stick of incense and passed it to her for her final round, the tip still blazing with fire.

"Let this circle shine like the stars and the moon," she said. "But let each of us shine with our own individual light." She blew the flame out, casting thick smoke into the nighttime air. "So mote it be."

"So mote it be."

Grimey called the quarters, his voice nervous and warbling. We had to steer him a little bit – he couldn't find the east at first, so we had to point him away from the violet shadow of the sun. But by the time he made it to the west and started invoking the spirits of water, he seemed more comfortable with the job. I watched his posture as he shifted from one direction to the next, calling in the spirits; with each turn he seemed to shed a little of whatever uncomfortable suit he'd worn into the circle.

We kept the ritual short – after all, there were only the three of us. After the quarters we talked for a little bit about Harvest Home, the second of the Harvest Festivals, the harvest of fruit (or was it grain?), after Lughnasadh and before Samhain. We talked about the Goddess and we thanked her for Her gifts; we talked about gods stalking through the fields and the forests. We listened for Pan's goat-steps in the grass.

And eventually, Lucy held took the athame and held it in her hand.

"You ready for the Great Rite?"

And I was.

The Great Rite is the most important part of any ritual, you see; it's this moment that represents the union of all things. The priestess holds the ritual knife, the athame, while the priest holds the chalice of wine. Then the priestess points the knife down at the cup, which tells the priest to say...

"As the athame is to the male..."

"So the cup is to the female," she replies.

And then in unison, they bring the athame and the chalice

together, dipping the blade into the wine. In that instant, all things spring into being, all creation and destruction, all our tears and our bile and our laughter, all the quantum possibility collapsing into reality in one triumphant orgasm of Goddess and God.

"And their union is the creation of the world."

So mote it be. So might it be. So I wish it would be.

I put the chalice to Lucy's lips. "Thou art Goddess," I said, and she drank the cheap wine that we had blessed with the kiss of the Goddess. "May you never thirst."

Her face puckered as she swallowed. "Thou art God," she said, suppressing a cough.

* * *

Grimey drove a black Buick made in the mid-80s. At first glance, it looked like a station wagon, but not really: something about it was off, like you were looking at the second picture in one of those 'What's the Difference?' puzzles in *Highlights*. Sometimes people didn't get it until you pointed out the shape of the tiny, tinted windows, the small metal lines near the rear. When they figured it out, every one of them would turn with a look somewhere between horror and absurd amusement and ask the same question. "Jesus Christ, Grimey," they'd say. "You drive a hearse?"

Grimey's hearse was decommissioned about six years ago. It was a piece of junk – as you'd expect, a hearse gets a lot of miles put on it, and whatever funeral parlor owned it apparently didn't keep up the maintenance – but that didn't matter to him. He loved the hearse despite the bad mileage and the rusted muffler, because he thought it reflected him: dark, but funny, in a bleak kind of way. Nobody else saw it like that. It reflected him, sure: much like its owner, the hearse really wanted to be dark and brooding, but just ended up being kind of awkward and hard to park.

The three of us were driving back from the Harvest ritual, rounding the curvy roads of Thousand Hills. Lucy was up front (at my insistence), while I sat in the back on the raised wooden platform upon which coffins once sat.

Grimey drove slowly – not that he had much choice, given the dead weight of his vehicle. I had driven it once, when we were moving to the new apartment, and it turned as though all the corpses the hearse had known were now grinding beneath its wheels.

Lucy had her head against the windows, and though I couldn't see her face, I knew she was staring at the stars. She lifted her head from the glass when we passed the NOW LEAVING THOUSAND HILLS sign. "So, Grimey," she began, "had you ever done a ritual before?"

Grimey shook his head. "No. Well, one." He took a hand from the wheel and brushed his greasy hair out from his forehead, then sat it back at nine o'clock. "When I was seventeen, I guess it was, I heard there was this open Full Moon. I snuck out of the house and borrowed my mom's car to go. I didn't get to do anything, though. No calling quarters or anything like that."

"Did you like it?" she asked.

"Sure," he said. "There were things I didn't get, and some of it was pretty cheesy – they did this thing where the priestess did the journey of the Goddess to the underworld and lost her clothes along the way. I kind of got the impression that was there because they liked the idea of the priestess getting naked and getting play-hit with a scourge." He pulled onto the highway back to town. "But there were a lot of people there, and they liked it, and I liked being around them. They told me about some books. I guess that's how I got started."

"But you only went there once?" Lucy shifted in her seat.

"Yeah, well. My mom found out about me sneaking out and she threw a fit, especially since she didn't believe me when I said

I'd gone out to the mall." He shrugged as though it weren't a big deal. "She grounded me, yelled about abusing her trust. By the time I had my own car, I was about ready to come up here, where there aren't any Full Moons. I never ended up going back."

Lucy frowned. "I guess your mom wasn't crazy about you being Pagan, huh?"

"She, uh, she doesn't know. I think." Grimey gripped the steering wheel a little more tightly. "I always made sure to keep my books locked up in my suitcase, and I never wear any of the jewelry or anything when I'm around her." He swallowed. "She's pretty Christian. You know how it is."

Except we didn't, Lucy and me. I mean, sure, we've had asshole relatives and strangers barking about witches our whole lives, but not our parents. We got into fights with them like everyone does, but not about religion. We never had to hide. Not like Grimey.

"That isn't right," Lucy said. "It's your life, your path. You shouldn't have to get somebody's approval to live the way you want to live, Grimey." She touched him on the arm. I saw that and felt an irrational annoyance with Grimey, as though Lucy only had a limited wellspring of affection and Grimey were draining it away.

Jealousy. It probably influenced what I said next.

"Lucy's right, man," I piped in. "I think you ought to tell your mom. As long as you keep it a secret, it's like there's something to be ashamed of – like *you* believe there's something to be ashamed of."

"Right, exactly," said Lucy. "That's the major barrier to accep-tance, you know? It's like being gay. Being closeted is safer, right? But if everyone's in the closet then nothing ever changes."

Grimey drummed on the steering wheel as we passed the fields of corn and cattle. "I don't know," he said. "I don't think she would take it well."

"You're a big boy, Grimey." I put my hand on his shoulder.

Solidarity. "She needs to learn to live with it. You're her son, she's can't go *too* crazy."

I watched Grimey's face in the rearview mirror. The light of the odometer flashed across his glasses. Soon a smile crossed his pasty face. "Maybe," he said. "Maybe you're right. I'll have to think about it."

Lucy smiled. I knew that smile from years of benevolent pranks: it said, "I have done good through mischief." Exactly what I had been looking for. Maybe Grimey was good for something after all.

* * *

We traded cars at the apartment – Grimey turned in for the night, and Lucy and I took her car over to Cheriton Valley. Lucy pulled into the parking lot and put the car into idle. Classic rock on the radio: I think it was Van Halen. The lights in the houses were all out already. My boys, and all the others like them, had already been put to bed. Only the flickering lights of televisions gave any sign of life.

"So which one is yours?" asked Lucy.

"3A. That one right there," I said, pointing two houses down from where we were parked. "Can you stay here for a minute? I need to go relieve Mike… He's a good guy, but you know, having company is against the rules. I don't think he cares, but—"

"Quit babbling." She poked me in the shoulder. "It's a stealth mission, I get it. I'll creep in once he's gone."

"Okay, okay." I popped open the door and lumbered out. "See you in a minute."

Mike was already waiting at the door when I walked in. "When I said I'd cover for you, Lou, I thought we were talking about, like, thirty minutes. I was supposed to be off an hour and a half ago."

"I know, I know," I said. "Sorry, man. I got held up."

He chuckled. "Yeah, I'll bet. You know, you could have just brought your lady-friend in with you. You know I'd never tell Dana."

"I know. I just felt like it would be awkward if it was obvious that you knew what I was up to." I walked back to the kitchen to grab my start-of-shift paperwork. "Besides, it's less fun if she knows you're a willing accomplice."

"So long as you remember that you owe me." He grabbed the doorknob, but stopped short of actually leaving. "Uh, hey, I know it's happy-fun-night, but I probably ought to tell you something."

I glanced up from the sign-in sheet. "Yeah? What's up?"

"Jimmy's mom's been calling. Hell if I know why – I'm not even sure Jimmy understands what the phone *is*. But you know how that crazy bitch gets. Minute I picked up she started screaming at me."

"What for?"

"I don't know. Said we were mistreating him or something. Putting bad ideas in his head, whatever that means. It was hard to tell – she's got that little old woman voice. I wanted to tell her that she needed to put her teeth in. Anyway, I've told her twice now that she's not allowed to talk to Jimmy, and that if she calls again I'm going to call the cops."

I rolled my eyes. "That's fucking great. Don't we have a restraining order on her or something?"

"Just a piece of paper. Don't mean a thing if you aren't scared of it. She probably doesn't think we have the balls to call the cops on her octogenarian ass." He shrugged and opened the door. "Anyway, just be on the lookout. I doubt she's gonna call this late, but it might happen in the morning. As for me, I'm going to the Dukum."

"Have a pint for me, huh?"

"You got it, chief." He took a step out and looked back. "Hey, just do me one favor. If you fuck on the couch, sanitize that shit."

"I'm not going to fuck anywhere that Donny's ass has been," I said. "Who knows what's happened there?" (Sadly, I did.)

"Whatever you say, man. My lips are sealed." He tipped an invisible hat. "Night, lady-killer."

I gave him a mocking sigh, and returned the gesture. "Night, Mike."

I got halfway through my paperwork before Lucy knocked at the window. I opened the door a crack and put my face in the margin. "What's the password?"

"I know where your parents keep the baby pictures."

I opened the door all the way. "Cheater."

"All's fair in love and war, kiddo." She put her hands on her hips and surveyed the living room: the couches and the television and the Formica coffee table. She turned around in a slow circle, taking the room in as though it were an art installation. "Geez, what a lifeless place," she said. "There isn't even anything on the walls."

"Donny used to have a wrestling poster, but he got mad one day and ripped it up," I said. "And Jimmy doesn't really have an appreciation for artwork, y'know?"

"Poor guy," she said. "He's the one who just kind of sits there?"

I nodded. "Yeah. Never says anything. I'm not really sure he's high-functioning enough for this environment sometimes... Sometimes the bosses talk about moving him to a hospital or something. Somewhere more controlled."

She sat down on the couch, right in Donny's spot. One more thing I couldn't save Lucy from. "You ever think about what it must be like for him? Going through life not really experiencing anything?" She twisted her lips into a sad and puzzled quirk. "You and Mike and whoever else all guide him around, feed him, take care of him... But he probably doesn't understand why you do it, or why his life is the way it is." She shook her head. "I think about it and I just think... What a gray way to live."

I sat down on the couch next to her, trying to think of a reassuring example – something to prove that Jimmy's life wasn't all bad. But I couldn't. Donny had a life – he held a job, he met people, he could even follow the plot of a wrestling match. His life had some variety – its good days and its bad days. But Jimmy's life wasn't like that; every day was the same for him. Get woken up, get fed, get sat on the couch until the next meal. Repeat until it's time for bed. An unending cycle, like a prayer wheel of monotony. The only interruptions were Jimmy's inexpressible urges, and I never could predict when one of those would surface.

Sometimes I wonder what it was like for him before... Donny had always been slow, but Jimmy used to be 'normal'. He'd been in the system for decades by the time I got assigned to the house, but I'd seen the files. Some kind of brain trauma when he was in his mid-twenties, though the files never got specific. Too far back.

Lucy poked me in the thigh.

"What?" I asked.

"You're being pensive," she said. Then, with a Cheshire grin, she said, "And you owe me a terrible movie."

"Right, right." I grabbed the remote and started flipping through the channels, all seventy-two of them. "You thinking contemporary schlock, or classic schlock?"

"See if you can find something with Vincent Price. I'm in a Vincent Price sort of mood."

We didn't find any Vincent Price movies on, or anything else from the golden age of B-movies. No appreciation for the old masters. We settled on the Sci-Fi Channel, which offered some sort of alien-saturated flick with acting so wooden it could have repopulated the rain forest. We came in late, after the titles, but that didn't matter – titles only matter for movies you're willing to admit you've watched.

When Lucy and I were eleven years old, we both got our own

televisions and our phones in our bedrooms. I remember the first movie we watched together: *Die, Monster, Die!*, a terrifically bad film based on an H.P. Lovecraft story. Andy had hung out in Lucy's room during it, and they would pass the phone back and forth. But Andy never really cared for horror or sci-fi; he liked Westerns. Lucy and I, though, we ate them up. About twice a month for years I would call her, or she would call me, and we'd turn on Sci-Fi or TNT or FX and laugh our way through the demise of some film student's hopes for respect.

Lucy still laughed at the rubber-faced aliens ("I think they just took a hair-dryer to a Nixon mask!") and moaned in disbelief at the plotting ("Did he *really* just run into the Birthing Chamber without putting on his radiation suit?") But something about it felt off to me. I laughed because she laughed, but only because she did.

Jesus. The last time we'd done this, I realized, was when we were sixteen, over five years ago. Somewhere in the fall of that year – October, now that I think about it, two weeks before Samhain – she'd called me up on a Saturday night and told me to turn to AMC. I remember the film: *Rosemary's Baby.* Neither of us had even seen it, but we'd heard of it: it was a classic, after all. Perhaps the most famous movie ever made about those loathsome, damnable witches.

We laughed at it the way our parents laughed at *The Wicker Man.* I remember Lucy mimicking Mia Farrow's desperate plea: "All that chanting through the wall? That's called an esbat! They use blood in their rituals!"

"That reminds me," I'd said. "Dad says we're running short on plump Christian babies this month. Could your mom pick some up before Full Moon?"

"Well, maybe," Lucy responded. "But they're hard to find fresh this time of year."

But we came to the end of the film. Rosemary walked through the secret door in her closet to the elderly couple's room. She saw the coven of witches, cooing over a baby in a black crib. An inverted cross hung above the child's crib. We saw the witches turn to Rosemary, that poor Catholic girl, and raise their hands in rapture.

"Hail Satan!" we heard them cry. "Hail Satan! The Year One has come!"

All the rumors had been true. The witches were real. They were like us: they had their esbats and sabbats, their rituals and their magick. But all that they did was in celebration of Satan, who raped and impregnated Rosemary, that poor waif.

We realized, silently and suddenly, that this was what the world saw when it heard about people like us, like our parents. This gruesome, ridiculous ceremony, this murder, this rape – they thought that was us.

And we didn't laugh at that.

"Lou!" said Lucy. A blue couch pillow smacked into my head. I jumped with a start. "Where is your head tonight, man?"

"What? What'd I miss?"

"The baby alien just burst out of that guy's skull. I swear to God, it looked like they'd microwaved a Peep and glued it to his forehead."

"Oh. I guess I missed it." I looked at the television and saw a hapless scientist running away from the Peep Monster. "Mind was somewhere else."

She turned the volume down. "What's on your mind, Philosopher?"

"I was thinking about when we used to do this, when we were kids," I said. I replaced the pillow on the couch. I moved it gingerly – I knew all the bodily fluids that had been spilled on that cushion over the years. "Why did we stop?"

She shrugged. "Mom got tired of us bogarting the phone all night, as I recall. She said if I needed to talk for that long all the time, I needed to start paying for a second line."

"Really? Was that all?"

"I think so. Why, what did you think?"

I shook my head. "I don't know. I just thought it was one of those things where one week we did and then we just... Forgot. Grew apart."

She smiled – the gentle smile, not the mischievous one – and ruffled my hair. "Don't be so serious, kid. Me and you, we're family. We don't grow apart."

Kid. Family. We don't grow apart. I was so sick of that thought. I guess I didn't put up a very good poker face, because Lucy noticed. "What?" she said. "What's wrong?"

"Luce... Look, is that what it is? Is that what you think of me as?"

She frowned. "Of course. What else would I think of you as?"

And that was when I stuck my tongue in her mouth.

To my everlasting horror, she gagged. She pulled back from the – well, 'kiss' might not be the right word, but that's what it was trying to be. She blinked at me and didn't say anything. I could feel the blood rising to the surface of my cheeks.

"Oh, Jesus," I mumbled. "I'm sorry."

"No, no, it's okay," said Lucy. She consoled me with a pat on the arm. Nurturing instinct. Goddamn it. "I'm – I'm glad I know, but, Lou, I don't – I never thought – Jesus."

A space marine screamed on the television as another of the Microwaved Peeps from Hell burned its way through his skull. The two of us sat there for a moment, silent.

"...look," she said, after a moment, "Don't worry about it. But I'm going to go. I mean, I need to drive to Columbia in the morning, and I need to look over my paper, and..."

"And suddenly staying the night here doesn't seem like such a hot idea."

She swallowed, and then shook her head. "No, Lou. I'm sorry." Then she brightened up, too obviously a front. "You know how it is, kiddo. Gotta put the C.V. first if you want to get ahead."

"You're right," I said, playing along. "Your paper. Right."

We got up and walked to the door. I opened it for her and followed her to the car. She unlocked the door and looked up.

"Grimey's probably out or asleep," I said. "Key is under the welcome mat of the apartment next door. Don't use the one under our mat, it doesn't work."

She started to get in the car, but paused and walked back to me. She gave me a hug, but our usual goodbye kiss noticeably moved from a peck on the lips to one on the cheek. "And thanks for putting me up for the night."

"Anytime," I said.

She got in her car and pulled out, drove away towards the Community Chest. I stood in the parking lot for a long moment, wishing I smoked so I would have some reason to keep standing there, watching for a phantom of Lucy's car.

"Fuck," I said, quietly, some moments later.

V

Dr. Eccleston looked over my draft with a frown. A *hrm* burbled its way up from his gut. He reached for a red pen and marked something in the margins. I tried to read it, but his loose script was impossible to read upside-down. I watched him from the other side of the desk from a hard orange McClain chair. My ass hurt.

He flipped the last page over, scanned the works cited, and set the paper down with a grunt.

"Well?" I asked.

He leaned back in his thick leather chair and looked at the ceiling. "I think that perhaps you should pick a different topic, Louis."

"What?" I frowned. "What do you mean?"

He gestured toward the paper. "It's not a bad draft. A little loose in the middle, but nothing that couldn't be fixed by a few hours of revision and maybe a trip to the Writing Center." He sat up and folded his hands on the desk. "But I've been watching your reactions to the material in class and in your homework..." I should note that this remark caught me off-guard. I would have bet a semester's tuition that he didn't actually read the homework.

"And?"

"And it seems that you've taken a shine to Julian the Apostate." Again, that word. The second syllable popped as he said it, and I heard disdain in the plosive. "There's nothing wrong with becoming fond of a historical figure, of course. Edward Gibbon loved Julian as well. But it's interfering with your objectivity. Your paper has a bit of the apologetic in it, as though you set your purpose to glorifying Julian from the outset, instead of critically examining his antagonism towards the church." He poured himself a cup of coffee from his tiny pot and stirred in a packet of Splenda. "There's a danger to writing about the men we admire. We forget their faults, romanticize them into better fitting our desires."

"And you think my paper is doing that?"

He sat his cup down and picked up the paper. "At least in places. Here, let me find it." He flipped through the pages until he found his spot, and then pushed the paper towards me. He had circled the last two paragraphs and scribbled words like *substantiate* and *unverifiable* in the margins. "Here, you say... What is it? 'History's course is rarely fixed, and sometimes is no more predictable than the flip of a coin,'" he quoted. "'Had Julian the Philosopher survived to have a reign as long as his uncle Constantine's, his reforms would likely have led to a Pagan renaissance in the Eastern Roman Empire. Just as Christianity prospered under Constantine, the traditional Roman religion would have bloomed under Julian. If his reign had been longer, if he had not chosen to campaign in Persian, it is likely that the Galileans would not have prevailed after all.'" He sat the paper down again. "It's a fairy tale, Louis. Completely unprovable, to begin with, and speculative to boot. Julian *did* die, and Paganism *did* fall. Things were too far gone to expect otherwise."

"Professor, I've heard the 'too far gone' line from every book I read for the draft," I said. "I think that's way too simple. I mean, Constantine raised Christianity from just another cult to the state religion. If he could do that for the Christians, why couldn't Julian have done it for the Pagans?"

"Have you studied the Reformation much, Louis?" He didn't actually wait for a response. "People left the Catholic Church because they were dissatisfied with many things in it. Well, of course, the Catholics noticed this, after a while, and they had the counter-reformation to try and get back some of their support. But they never really recovered from it. Certainly they never brought all those Protestants back into the fold. And the Catholics had better organization than the Pagans ever did." He sat up, folded his hands on the desk. "When people leave a faith, it's very hard to get them to come back."

"So forty years is really all it took, you think? A religion that had been around for centuries could just be displaced forever by a few decades of neglect?"

He shrugged. "It was a Pagan world for a long time, yes. But we grew out of it."

We grew out of it. Like when you were seven and thought you were going to be an astronaut. "Are we going to grow out of the Christian world, too, Professor?"

He smiled, but it was a would-you-please-get-out-of-my-office-you-little-shit sort of smile. "Some would say we already have. I think that's overselling it, personally." He slid my paper all the way to me and stood up. "It's up to you. If you turn in this paper and it's at the level I expect it would be at after revision, I think it will be fine. But... I think you should take a hard look at your work and think about how it fits in with your goals as a scholar. I think you can find something more suitable to write about. This was only the first draft, after all – you still have plenty of time." His smile shifted, became a little more genuine. "For what it's worth, I think Julian's a fascinating man too. After all the bloodshed and in-fighting the sons of Constantine brought to the empire, it was nice to have an intellectual on the throne. The Romans thought so at the time, too. But oftentimes, our heroes are the very worst people to write about."

I nodded and took the paper back. "Thanks, Professor."

"You're welcome, Louis. I'm sorry we couldn't talk longer—" no, you weren't, you lying fuck "—but I have to rush. Department meeting."

I followed him out into the hallway and watched him lock up. "Really? What's on the agenda today?"

"Oh, the usual," he said. "Administration, grants, tenure review." He pocketed his keys and started down the hall to the meeting room. "Anything in the world but religion!" he called over his shoulder.

* * *

Grimey's mother darkened our doorstep around three PM on the second Saturday after the incident with Lucy. (I was handling it well, except for the occasional spasm of writhing mortification.) She pulled up in her sea-green minivan, a holdover from when Grimey was younger. She had really wanted to be a soccer-mom, you could tell; she had invested in the minivan hoping to shuttle Herman and all his little friends around. He would play in all the leagues, and she could watch him making shots and blocking goals and doing whatever the hell kids who play sports did. Meanwhile she could sit in the stands in a sun-dress and big sunglasses, gossiping with others of her ilk. The American Dream. Too bad she had an inside kid.

Anyway. I saw her park her minivan next to Grimey's hearse and get out. She wore jeans and a magenta sweater, wore her brown hair up in a sort of bouffant. She didn't smile as she approached the door.

"Hey, Grimey!" I called. No answer. I walked down the hall and heard the shower going. Typical. "Hey, Grimey!" I called again and rapped on the bathroom door.

"What?" he said, voice muffled by the hollow wooden door.

"Your ma is here."

"Let her in. I'll be out in a second."

The doorbell rang and I opened the door for her. Grimey's mom is a short woman, shorter than me or Grimey by a head, but she has a presence about her that makes both of us shrink a couple inches whenever she's nearby. Around her neck she had a small golden cross, not gaudy at all. "Hi, Mrs. Hemphill. Gr..." I paused and realized I'd always just called him *Grimey*, even in the rare occasions I'd had to talk to his mom. She'd never called me on it. Then again she'd never paid me much mind in the first place. Should I call him Herman? Should I just call him Grimey?

Grimey's mom looked at me expectantly. "Yes?"

"He's in the shower. He'll be right out."

I led her into the living room, which Grimey had made uncomfortably tidy the night before. He got so obsessive about it I was afraid he'd started using amphetamines. All of the ramshackle friendliness of our furniture had been straightened up, but it doesn't matter how much you dust cheap old college furniture – shit still looks like shit. Now we just looked like we were uncomfortable with having shitty furniture.

"Can I get you anything?" I asked.

"A glass of water would be fine," she said. I got it for her, and she remained silent otherwise. No questions about my classes, or whether I'd found a girlfriend, or what kinds of clubs I was in. I found something admirable about that. I mean, sure, I was getting the cold shoulder, but I can appreciate people who don't mire themselves in small talk. I was not a significant item in her universe, and that was fine by me.

Grimey came out of the shower a few minutes later, hair free of oil, wearing the stainless red Dobson Hall t-shirt he'd gotten during Freshman Week and kept sequestered in the back of his closet for when he needed camouflage. Glad to see you're not hiding anymore, Grimes.

"Hi sweetie," said his mom, and she pulled him into a tight hug and kiss on the cheek. As usual, she didn't acknowledge I was in the room at all as she did this; her eyes were only for him. Grimey shot me an embarrassed grin and kissed her on the forehead.

"Hi mom," he said. "How was the drive?"

"Awful. The road was full of maniacs, people going 75 miles an hour the whole way. No wonder there's so many accidents."

"Oh?" I said, breaking into the bubble of maternal affection. "Did you see many accidents on the way?"

She blinked as though she had forgotten I was in the room.

"Well, no. But you hear about them."

"Ah, right," I said. The hypothetical accidents caused by hypothetical maniacs driving five miles above the not at all hypothetical speed limit. "I'm gonna get out of here, Grimes. I've got my thing to go to." I had no 'thing', but nobody deserves to have a roommate hanging around when his mom is in town.

Grimey looked relieved. "Uh, right. And then you have work later, right?"

"Yeah. See you in the morning."

I busted up as soon as I got to the car. Poor fucker. He'd still be squirming for days after she left.

* * *

I took over the house from Dana that night without much fanfare: same cigarette on the front porch, same half-hearted salute. She didn't even come back inside once I'd gone in. Her paperwork was already filled out and filed, and she'd even left mine on the counter, an uncapped pen waiting for my signature. I guess she was antsy to get out. Why, though? I mean, where the fuck did Dana have to do with her time?

The boys were in good moods – well, good moods for them, anyway. Donny camped out in front of the television and watched cartoons. I filled out my paperwork and then flopped into the easy chair in the living room. I'd had little to feel happy about the past couple of weeks, but the boys had been good. Times like that, I felt like I had a pretty good job, one that didn't even feel like a job. More like being a big brother, taking care of the kids while the parents were away.

I didn't recognize the show they were watching, and it looked entirely too bright and cheerful for my tastes. But it kept Donny entertained, so I let it be.

Jimmy just sat, watching the wall. He had his groove in the couch and his spot on the wall, and he spent most of his life in them.

Looking at him then, I couldn't help but think of what Lucy said about him. *What a gray way to live.* People always wrote about how easy Jimmy was to take care of. The guy I replaced still lived in town, and occasionally I'd run into him in at Hy-Vee. "Donny's such a troublemaker," he'd say. "But that Jimmy, a peach."

But I would have rather had Donny any day. Donny was rowdy, sure, but *people* were rowdy. People get upset when they don't get their way. People get frustrated when their favorite TV show isn't on, or if you make hamburgers when they want spaghetti. Jimmy didn't do any of those things. The only difference between him and a coma patient was that he kept his eyes open.

I don't know why, but I felt compelled to talk to him, then. I knew he couldn't understand me. But for some reason, I had to try. "Hey, Jimmy?" I said. "Hey, buddy. Look at me."

Jimmy roused slightly and twitched his eyebrows. Almost a frown.

"How are you feeling, Jimmy?" I asked. I said it slowly. He didn't respond, but his eyes moved – maybe recognition, maybe just my mind seeing what it wanted to see. "Are you hungry, pal? Do you want me to make you—"

Someone pecked at the door – sharp notes struck on the glass with a key. I checked my watch and saw that it was 9:23. Nobody ever visited the boys that late. I grimaced at Jimmy. "Uh, hold that thought, bud. Let me see who's at the door." It was probably Maggie, working over in 3C. She always lost her pens and needed to come by to filch them from us...

I opened the door and saw an old woman in a dress too stuffy and ugly to be anything but handmade, her vulture-face pulled into a frown. Before any of that registered the smell hit me. *Essence of Wilting Violets.*

"Uh, hello?" I said. I didn't know who she was. "Can I help

you?"

"I'm here for my son," she said, deadpan. She looked over my shoulder into the living room. "Jimmy, the one on the couch."

Oh, shit.

"Mrs. Everett?" I asked. "Jimmy's mother?"

"Yes, that's who I am," she said. Her high voice was cracked and aged. "Now get out of my way. I'm taking my boy back home, where he belongs."

No, no, no. The reports never said specifically what happened to Jimmy, but we're not idiots. We knew exactly how he'd gotten hurt. When he first came to us, he had been in traction – covered in bruises and contusion, two cracked ribs, even a broken leg. He'd fallen down the stairs, the report said. But we knew better. He was a ward of the state because he had been pushed.

"Look, you can't do that. You can't even visit him this late – he's supposed to be in bed in a few minutes."

"I'm not taking him on any visits." She was very matter-of-fact, her course fixed. "I have thought this over and over for as long as you all have had him. Locked up here in some state house – this ain't a way for a person to live." She locked her vulture eyes to mine. "I'm taking him home. That's that."

Donny bounded over to the door. "Hi, miss!" He looked back at Jimmy. "Hey, Jim! Company!"

Jimmy looked at the door, his head cocked slightly.

I looked at Donny, giving him the barest this-is-serious-leave-this-to-me stare I could muster. "Donny, go to your room, okay, buddy?" I said.

He looked at me with hurt eyes. Donny's feelings bruise like peaches. I promised I'd make it up to him later, somehow. "What?" he said. "But why?"

"Just do what I tell you, okay?" I said. Fuck, Donny, this was not the time...

He looked like he was about to argue, but, thank God, he cooperated and stumbled off to his room.

"How long are you planning to stand there? Get out of my way," said Mrs. Everett. "Jimmy! Come on, we're going."

Jimmy rose to his feet and took a few slow steps toward the door. I did my best to stay between him and his mother. But...

But I couldn't touch him.

It's the first rule of the job. You can't touch them. You're not a cop, not a doctor, not a relative. If they want to go, you do whatever you can to stop them. Whatever you can, except touch them. If he wanted to go, I couldn't stop him. I could only try to reason with him, and reasoning with Jimmy was like reasoning with a four-year-old. (Fuck. *Still* shouldn't think of him like that. Still not working out so well.)

So that left the mother. She was an autonomous person, right? She could be talked to. Right?

"You know why Jimmy's here instead of at home with you, Mrs. Everett," I said. "You aren't his guardian. You haven't got a right to do this." I swallowed. "I will call the police if you don't leave now. Do you really want to go to jail now, at your age?"

She ignored me. She slipped her tiny, bone-thin frame past me and into the living room.

"This is kidnapping, Mrs. Everett. You are committing the felony crime of kidnapping. If you leave now, I'll ignore it and we can forget about this." I was lying, of course, spewing every bullshit line I could think of. I'd call Dana and by the morning the old bat would be arrested if she got within a thousand feet of 3A.

Assuming I could stop her.

"The car's double-parked, Jimmy," she said. "Listen to your mother."

He came when she called, a child called to his mother's voice.

I wanted to grab him by the shoulders. I wanted to shout at him. *If you go, it will be the death of you.*

And I could tell you that I thought about what she could say, if I did that, what she could tell the cops, the Kirksville Daily Express. Attendants manhandling their patients. Rampant abuse in Cheriton Valley. She could get me fired. Maybe prosecuted. I could tell you that, because I did think about all of those things.

I could tell you that I thought about Jimmy, and what would happen to him. No medicine. Nobody qualified to treat him if he had an accident. The possibility that this woman – this woman who had already ruined him – could, in her quiet, sullen madness, kill him. Because I thought about that, too.

But my thoughts were mainly focused on one question: *What am I willing to do to resolve this?* And the answer, to my shame, was simply this: *Not enough.*

"Jimmy," I pleaded. "Listen to me, buddy. Please."

"This isn't your job, kid," she said, her voice somewhere between snarl and sympathy. "He's my son, not yours. He's just a meal ticket to this company you work for. He deserves better."

She glared at me, then motioned to Jimmy. He followed her outside, and I followed him. "Jimmy – Jimmy, come back. I'll make you ice cream and you won't be in trouble. Just come back in." She opened the door to the car. "Do you remember what happened the last time you ran away? Do you remember all the drugs we had to fill you full of?" I swallowed. "For gods' sake, Jimmy, don't make me do that again."

He looked at me, then. He actually looked at me, right in the eyes. He looked sorry. He looked as though he knew this would end badly for him. That he would be going off his meds and have his symptoms flare up. That his mother would berate him, would beat him, would be the end of him. That when we found him – *if* we found him – we would have to punish him, commit him to some asylum where he'd never know the comforts of home again. Not for vindication. Just because they could never trust that it wouldn't happen again.

But it was his mother. What was he supposed to do?

This – all of this – it was just in my head. I was projecting thoughts onto him that he had lost all capacity for years ago. But it's what I saw. That's all I know.

Then Jimmy got into his mother's station wagon, and soon, they were gone.

* * *

Dana sent me home at five that morning, after hours of paperwork and phone calls. ("You've done enough tonight," she said.) The police hadn't found Jimmy or any sign of his mother. They put out a teletype for the license plate, but no hits. They could already be in Indiana, for all we knew.

I kept running it over in my head – what I could have said, what I could have done. And short of grabbing a woman in her seventies by her brittle shoulders and throwing her out of the house, I couldn't think of anything. That didn't make me feel any better. I should have been braver, more clever, more... Something.

And I doubted I would have a job for much longer.

It was still dark when I pulled into the Community Chest. The lights were out in every apartment but one – mine. I frowned. Had Grimey forgotten to turn out the lights? I opened the door to my car and got my answer – black metal blasting from the open window. "Motherfucker," I said. I was surprised the cops weren't outside our door for a peace disturbance. I tramped upstairs to our apartment, intent on murdering him.

"Grimey!" I yelled, slamming the door open so hard a mirror fell off the wall and bounced onto the carpet. I got no reply except for a hideous metal scream, the kind that starts somewhere around the eighth circle of Hell and works its way up.

Our whole apartment was trashed. Books, *my* books, everywhere, the trashcan knocked over, shards of a broken beer bottle behind the couch. I slammed my fist against the stereo's power button and listened for any sound of him. "Grimey, where the fuck are you?"

No answer, again.

I looked in the kitchen – not there. Not in the bathroom. Only one place to look, then. I found him sprawled on the floor in his bedroom, an empty bottle of Boone's Farm and conspicuous blue stain on the carpet next to him. The room stank, a noxious concoction of alcohol and pot.

He groaned when I flipped on the lights. "Lou?"

"What the fuck happened here?"

"M'sorry, man." He looked at me with bleary eyes. "I'll... I'll clean it up in the morning."

"Your 'in the morning' can kiss my ass. This place is a wreck."

He struggled up to a sitting position. "Things didn't go so well with my mom..." He sighed. "I dunno. I got really drunk."

I snapped. "Do I look like I give a fuck about your mommy problems? If you had any clue – any fucking *clue* – of what I've been through tonight..." I paused, let out a deep, angry breath. "Jesus. Get the fuck up and put this place back together."

He ran his fingers through his oily hair, the haze seeming to lift a little. "Hey, fuck you," he said, his voice still slurred from alcohol. "You don't have a right to just barge in here and start making demands—"

"The hell I don't. This is my fucking apartment too, you leech, and I'm sick of coming home to see my shit all over the place and listening to your bullshit excuses."

He stood up and brought his face within two inches of mine. The smell of sour whiskey filled my nose. More than anything, I wanted to punch him. "'Leech?' You cocksucker," he spat. "You know what *I'm* tired of? You and your fucking superiority complex. You thinking you're so much better than everybody else. Lou fucking Durham, savior of the fucking universe."

For a moment he really did look intimidating. Probably the only time in Grimey's life all the black clothes and chains made him look like he really could beat somebody's ass. Too bad he wasn't sober enough to enjoy it.

"I'm not putting up with this." I caught myself and took a few steps back. "Fine. Go back to sleep, asshole, and fix the goddamn apartment when you don't look so pathetic."

He pushed past me, mashing his shoulder into my chest, and went out into the hallway. I followed him, rubbing my clavicle. "Grimey? What are you doing?"

"I'm not gonna sit down and listen to your bullshit. I've got too much on my mind…" He fished his keys out of his pocket. "I gotta think things through. I gotta figure out what I'm going to do about my mom. I'm going out."

"'Out?' Where? It's like, six in the morning. Where are you going to go?"

"*Out.*" He made for the door.

"Woah, Grimes, hold up, man," I said. Even in my red fog, I knew this was a bad idea. "You're sauced, you're not driving anywhere."

"You're not my fucking mother," he said. I watched him from the front stoop as he got into his car and started it up. I rolled my eyes as he turned on the headlights and started to pull away.

Asshole. I had no idea why I put up with him for so long, when he was nothing but a whiny momma's boy who didn't know the first thing about—

I heard a very loud crash and, completely on instinct, ran out the door. The sun was just starting to rise, bathing the neighborhood in a ghostly tableau of violet ground and rusty sky. I rushed down the street in the direction of the noise. The elm tree at the entrance to the Community Chest had been knocked backwards, its roots still clinging to the dripping earth. Wrapped around the trunk of the tree was the grille to Grimey's hearse.

VI

The nurse was drawing blood when I found Grimey's room. I looked away. I didn't want to see his fluids. It felt so invasive, like catching him masturbating. The nurse must have noticed, because when she finished, she called to me. "All done," she said, in that sort of high, flighty voice nurses develop from working with children and those who regress into children at the sight of a needle. "You can come on in."

"Thanks," I said. I walked into a room the color of sterility and fluorescence and took a look at him. He was pale, even for Grimey. Practically exsanguinated. I'm sure the color would have appealed to him on most occasions. Two black eyes, one of his legs elevated and wrapped. A neck brace. The chart on his bed listed some of the injuries: concussion, two black eyes, a number of broken bones. Internal bleeding. And, almost an afterthought, whiplash.

The nurse took the blood away and left us alone in the room. We looked at each other for a moment before I finally summoned the nerve to talk. "Hey, buddy," I said, softly.

"Hey," he said.

"You going to be okay?"

He tried to shrug, but he only made it as far as a wince. "I guess. I'm not dead. They tell me that's something."

"You did a number on that tree. I'm pretty sure your hearse has seen the last of its days."

"That fucking hearse," he muttered. "Didn't even have airbags. Cheap-ass morticians."

We looked at each other for a moment in silence.

"What?" I asked.

"Aren't you gonna say something? Ask what happened?" He coughed so hard that my throat started hurting too. "Anything?"

"I didn't think you'd want to talk about it. Especially after what we said before." I took a breath. "Okay, so what happened?"

"My mom. I told her. I mean, about the Wicca and stuff, like you and Lucy told me to."

"And?" I asked.

"And she… She started yelling at me. And crying. She said she'd been turning a blind eye to the chains and the goth stuff for years, hoping it would just be a thing I grew out of, but that this witch shit was too much for her." He looked down. "She said I was just doing it to fuck with her. That she didn't deserve to be treated like that." He looked back at me, and his face – always too chubby to be properly dark and intriguing like he wanted – now looked grotesque, hollow, a choleric mask on a sanguine frame. "She said nobody ever became a witch for any reason besides hating their parents."

"That's not true, Grimes," I whispered. "You know that's not true."

He was quiet for a long time. "Maybe *you* know it's not true, Lou. Me, I don't think I know anything right now." He took a drink from a sippy-cup on the counter next to him. "She said I wasn't her son anymore, not until I got my life in order, not until I came back to Jesus. And she doesn't pay tuition for other people's children." He sat the cup back down, and muttered, "Or their health insurance either, I'm guessing."

I began to see the gravity of the situation. "I'm… Look, I'm sorry, Grimey. And I know that's about as lame as apologies get, but… I'm sorry. I had a bad, bad night at work. When I got home, I took it out on you."

He didn't say it was okay, but I didn't really expect him to. "I don't know what the fuck I'm going to do, man. When I get out of here, I mean."

"You'll be okay. You'll figure something out." I patted him on the arm. "Don't get too worked up. That's just the morphine talking."

"Shit," he said. "Morphine's the only thing worth looking forward to."

* * *

I didn't go to class for two days. My work week had ended (probably forever) on Sunday morning, so I didn't go to work, either. I sat around the apartment, waiting for the phone to ring. Waiting to hear that Grimey and Jimmy were coming home, at last.

The phone never rang.

For two days I sat on the couch, on the floor, on the bed, stood in the corner, stood with my forehead pressed to the crack in the bathroom door. For days I barely ate and never slept.

At nine AM on Wednesday – I remember, because I had been staring on the clock in the living room for an hour – I realized that my internal monologue had shut off. The little life-script I wrote as I went through the day, the voice that reassured me of control over my own brain – it just wasn't there. I had been staring at walls and feeling nothing, thinking nothing. My brain was a blank screen. The past week had forced me off the goddamned air. I didn't even go into reruns.

At noon on Tuesday, the phone rang. I pounced on it like it was a sleepy gazelle. "Hello?" I said, the first time I'd spoken in twenty hours.

"Lou?" Dana. "Hey. How are you?"

"I'm..." Fucked up? Not sleeping? Worried that Jimmy is dead and Grimey is crippled? Wishing I had money for a new liver and liquor to ruin it with? "I'm fine. What's up?"

"Not much has changed," she said. "We think Mrs. Everett might have gone down to Macon or Moberly. The police are keeping in touch, but the she must have been planning this for a while."

"That's pretty methodical," I said. "I wouldn't have expected

77

it out of her."

"Makes two of us." She hesitated. Come on, Dana, just get it out. Was I fired? Was I being arraigned? "My supervisor wants to have a hearing with you. With us. Make sure that you didn't do anything to agitate Jimmy. We don't want to be liable for anything."

"How could we be liable? I mean, his mom kidnapped him. Who could sue us?"

"Jimmy's sister in La Plata, maybe. She's his power of attorney. I don't think she would, but... But you know how people are. If she sees the chance to bilk us for a few grand, she'll take it."

"But I followed the rules," I said. "I did what I was supposed to do."

"I'm sure you did," she said. I didn't believe her. "It's just a hearing. Don't let it worry you too much."

I stared at the white wall of the kitchen. "Fine. When?"

"Friday afternoon. Will that work?"

"Yes," I said. "I'm guessing I don't need to show up to work until then."

She didn't answer at first, but I could picture her slow nod. "Right. Yes."

"Okay."

"I'll call you if we hear anything else about Jimmy. I'll see you Friday." And she hung up.

I held the phone for a long time and stared at the wall. Outside I could hear somebody's dog barking. No other sounds. When the dog stopped, I found myself unsure as to whether it had really been there, or if I'd hallucinated it.

Hallucinations. I've heard that it doesn't take long without sleep before that starts to happen to you...

I flipped through my phonebook and came to Lucy's name. I needed to talk to someone – needed to get my head back on straight. Needed somebody to convince me to go to bed. I called her and listened for the rings.

One, two, three, four rings. Five. Click.

"Hi! You have reached the voicemail of Lucy Walstead. I'm probably in class at the moment, but if you leave me a message I'll get back to you. Blessed be!" Beep.

Fuck.

"Luce, it's Lou. Could you call me back when you get this? It's important. A lot of shit has happened over the past couple of days and… Look, I just really need to talk to you. Please." I paused, wondered whether it would be best to give her a summary of Shit That Had Gone Wrong in the voicemail itself. No, probably not. Better to lay it out once than have to explain it again when she called. "Thanks in advance. Bye." Click.

I put my phone back in my pocket and made myself a grilled cheese sandwich. I was surprised I had the hand-eye coordination for it. I took a bite and realized the middle was still stone cold, but I ate it anyway.

It only took another hour of blank staring before I finally went to bed. I closed the blinds in my room and undressed and fell on the mattress, surrendering myself to blessed darkness.

And like clockwork, the phone rang just as I pulled the blanket over my body.

I fumbled into my pants pocket and grabbed the phone, almost missing the call. (I knew because David Bowie had almost gotten to the second *"Alright!"* in the chorus to *Young Americans*.) "Lucy?"

"Ah, no, I'm afraid not, Louis." Of course not. The ring hadn't been *Sweet Jane*, had it? The voice on the other end was an older man. He sounded authoritative, but soft.

"Sorry. Uh, who is this, then?"

"It's Dr. Eccleston. Is this a bad time?"

Eccleston? How the fuck did he get my phone number? (*From the student directory, dumbass.*) "No, no, Professor. This isn't a bad time. What do you need?"

"I noticed you weren't in class yesterday, and, well, I'd heard about Herman. He's your roommate, isn't he?"

"Yes, sir."

"Louis, you know you don't have to call me sir..." *Trust me, says the purple sweater. Trust me. I'm your friend.* "Would you be willing to come by my office today? I want to talk to you about some things."

"Does it need to be today? I was just about to take a nap – I haven't really slept well in the past few days."

"Of course, of course," he said, in his kind old uncle voice. "I understand. This must have been hard on you. Tomorrow, maybe?"

"Sure. Tomorrow. Tomorrow is fine. What time?"

"Whenever works for you," he said.

"Alright. After the usual class time? Is that okay?"

"That's fine. Get some rest, Louis."

"Thank you, Professor."

We hung up, and I dropped the phone on the floor next to my bed. I found myself staring up at the ceiling, completely unable to shut my eyes.

Of *course* he would be the one to call.

* * *

Dr. Eccleston looked itchy. Probably the sweater. A violet wool sweater today, with big green cables of wool. The office lamps glinted off his bald pate and I found myself thinking of the cheesy lighting in *Attack of the Mutant-Space Peeps*. He had the shade down on his window, so even though it was early in the afternoon, no natural light filtered into the room. He shuffled around some papers, not really looking at them. I guess he didn't really want to have this conversation either, but it was too important to his Protestant ethics to let it go.

"So, Louis. Obviously Herman must be on your mind..." He looked at me with a sad, embarrassed smile. "That's such a silly thing for me to say. 'Obviously…' Having a roommate in that situation. I can only imagine the difficulty." He turned around and took down the coffee pot from his shelf. "Can I offer you a cup?"

"Thanks," I said. He poured me a mug and gave me two sugars and half-and-half. I took a drink before I thought to see what the mug said. *Corpus Christi Baptist Church.* Of course. Eccleston drank out of a white-and-purple Truman State mug, himself. The coffee was good, at least.

"Are you and Herman close?" he asked.

"Yeah," I said. "I mean, we've lived together for years now. We'd have to be."

Eccleston held his coffee mug with both hands and considered his words. "I heard that he had tried to hurt himself. That he hit the tree on purpose. Did he say anything to you about that?"

"Professor, with all due respect," – which is what, exactly? – "that's kind of personal, isn't it? I mean, Gri—Herman has a right to his privacy."

He nodded and sat his cup down. "Well, yes, of course. I just wanted to know because… Well, you know as well as I do. Herman is a member of my church, beyond being a former student. I feel somewhat responsible for his well-being."

A member of your church? And you, dutiful shepherd, looking after the flock. "Right." He didn't say anything. I guess he expected that I would volunteer more information. I stared into the darkness of his coffee and frowned. "Professor, who told you that? About Grimey wanting to hurt himself."

"Grimey?" he asked with a frown. "Is that a nickname?"

"Yeah," I said. "It's short for Grimalkin."

The frown didn't disappear, but Eccleston didn't press the issue."I called Herman's mother when I heard he was in the hospital. When she went to Truman, she went to my church too. We've kept in touch, off and on, through the years. She said that he had been having some problems, things he wouldn't talk to her about. Which led her to believe he might have been willing to hurt himself." He shrugged. "You know how things are. We thought perhaps Herman had shared things with you he wouldn't share with us." He leaned forward, placing his hand, palm down, on the desk. "We just want to help him."

You want me to be an informant, I thought. *Trust his mother, and trust his preacher. Tell us everything you know. Bring him back to us.*

"I'm sorry, Dr. Eccleston. I just don't think it would be right to talk about this without Grimey knowing. If he was having problems, those are his to address, not mine."

He looked disappointed, but he nodded. "Well, perhaps, though if he is a danger to himself..." He sighed. "But I understand your position, of course. Perhaps once he gets out of the hospital you can talk to him about it.

"In the meantime, though, I wanted to talk to you about our class..."

Really? He was bringing up schoolwork?

He sat up straighter, subtly stretched his neck. Shifted from Kindly Preacher to Understanding Professor. "Well, having something like this happen to a friend is an awful experience. When I was a young man, I remember hearing about an old girlfriend who had tried to swallow a bottle of sleeping pills... Terrible." He shook his head in that way everybody does when they try to demonstrate how well they understand your pain, but they don't. They can't.

"Anyway. I know you're in distress right now, and when Herman comes home, you will probably be helping him recover. I understand that is a lot to go through, and I just want you to know that, ultimately, my class is just not all that important." He took a drink from his Truman State mug and leaned back. "Take as much time as you need on the paper, or on anything, really. For that matter, I'd be happy to give you an incomplete and let you finish the work over the holidays or in the spring. It would be callous for me to do otherwise."

I took another drink of the coffee and thought about it.

Sharing a drink might be one of the world's few true universal traditions. When we drink together, we create a bond that goes deeper than a contract or a promise. We drink at weddings in gladness; we drink at wakes in grief. It's a ritual, like eating, like sex.

I picture myself passing the chalice to Lucy at Midsummer. I hold the wine to her lips and she drinks. *May you never hunger,* I whisper. *May you never thirst.* I kiss her, and she tastes like the Goddess.

How many times have I sat in this office, watching you drink your coffee, never offered a cup? And today we share a drink. Is this our communion, Professor? I share my grief with you, and you grant me your understanding and your sympathy. A little bit of magick between us, a spell cast in these bitter grounds.

I sat there, looking at the coffee. Dr. Eccleston said nothing. Maybe he thought I would cry. Maybe he thought I was entering a stoic torpor, the culturally acceptable white male variant of crying.

You're trying to save me, aren't you? You'll do what you can for Grimey, sure. But Grimey's too far gone, now. He'll never be the same. But me... Maybe you can pull me back from the precipice.

I remembered the dream I had, just before Grimey and I went to visit Eccleston's church. The feeling of boiling lead on my skin, the hot rods stabbed into my side. It's funny; I had never been much one for the dreamy, psychedelic part of Paganism. I devoted myself to Thoth, to Hermes, to Athena, Odin; gods of reason, gods of analysis. I never put stock into dreams or prophecy. But I remembered every sensation of that dream. Every moment on the rack. Every drip of burning lead...

How much easier it would be just to give over your scriptures. How much easier to renounce your heretical ways. You wouldn't have to die, or be persecuted. Your parents wouldn't disown you. Your children would never be taken away from you by the government. Your friends wouldn't tell you that you're going to hell. You could cheer for Rosemary. You could boo the witches. You could join the Fellowship of Christian Athletes. You could vote Republican.

No need to fear anymore – the fear, every day, of being found out, of being judged. You could even tell the triumphant story of how you turned away from evil, left behind your wicked past, accepted the One True Way. They'd put you on talk shows. You could be Born Again.

You – I – could be a hero. I could come out of the darkness and enter the light.

How much easier it would be, to be an apostate.

"Louis?" asked Dr. Eccleston. "Are you alright?"

"Professor," I said, at last, "do you remember the day when Grimey and I came to your church, a few weeks ago?"

He nodded. "I saw you in the crowd, yes."

"Do you know why we were there?"

He shook his head. "I assumed Herman came for the service, as he does, sometimes. I imagined you were just curious."

"I guess that's one way of putting it." I sat his cup down. "I didn't believe Grimey at first when he said you were a pastor. I wanted to see what you said in your sermons, how different it was from the classroom."

He lowered his gaze, and his speech came slow and uncertain. "And?"

"And it isn't any different at all. In class, all you talk about is about the inexorable rise of Christianity – how we outgrew that old world and grew into a new one, like Western Civilization finally hit puberty. Julian the Apostate is as much of a passing cloud to you as he ever was to Athanasius." He started to break in, but I wouldn't let him. I talked over him, the furor rising in my voice. "And you said the same thing in church that Sunday.

People turn away from Christianity, and you told your people just to give them time – because eventually, Christ is going to win their hearts back. Because he has to. Because we can't escape Him.

"Grimey and I, we didn't go to your church because we wanted to hear about Jesus. We went because we wanted to know our enemies. Grimey's never been a member of your church. He came to appease his mother. Probably to appease you, too, I guess. But in his heart, he doesn't belong to you. He belongs to the Goddess."

Eccleston's expression grew more and more bewildered as that all spilled out of me. When I finished, he caught himself, and stammered out a response. "The 'Goddess?'"

"Yes," I said. "He's a Pagan. So am I."

He blinked, then leaned back in his chair. "I didn't know that," he said, carefully. "Neither did his mother, apparently."

"Of course not," I said. "When he told his mother, she disowned him. That's why he drove his car into the goddamn tree."

"That's horrible," said Dr. Eccleston. "Louis – Lou, if I had known about it, I would have..."

"You would have what? Tried to talk him into coming back to the fold? Told him about sin and redemption, tried to get him to throw away his pentagram and put on a cross?" I stood up, and Eccleston, perhaps unknowingly, shrunk back – I wonder if he thought I was going to attack him. No, no – I was angry, sure, more angry than I'd ever been in my life. Just not like that.

But I was in the neighborhood.

"You think you're inevitable, but you're not," I said, finally. "I don't need you to save my soul."

I grabbed the door handle and walked into the hall. Behind me I heard Eccleston get up from his desk and start after me, but I didn't stop to look. "Lou, wait!" he called. "Wait!"

I didn't. I walked out of the gaudy shadows of McClain Hall

and out into the cold autumn daylight.

Dazed. Maybe that's the word to describe how I felt as I walked across the brick mall in front of McClain. Other students hustled to class, walked to the library, laughed or grumbled or threw the last Frisbee of the year. Early October. Halfway through the fall – a threshold of sorts. Soon it would be Samhain, when the old ghosts are close enough to touch...

I shook my head and turned away from the quad. I walked back toward McClain. I passed through the alley between that hall and the one next to it and stopped three quarters of the way through. I looked up and realized that the office above me – the one with the drawn shades... That was Dr. Eccleston's office. Wasn't it? Somehow I'd never thought of the geography of the building before; the rooms inside never connected to the rest of the world, for some reason. But no, there was just this one little barrier between in there and out here. One thin, fragile pane of glass.

There was a fist-sized chunk of concrete in the alley's debris. I picked it up, felt the weight of it in my hands. I ran my fingers across the surface. I took in all of the grooves, the pockmarks, the holes. All of the tiny imperfections that would have driven Plato mad.

Plato used this narrative, and all his descendents used it too – Aristotle and Aquinas, and all their children, right down to Joseph Campbell and James Frazer. The human race began as savages, believing in savage gods: the primitive deities of the ignorant, entities who must be paid in blood and superstition. And eventually we turned from that to polytheism – but polytheism was merely savagery in disguise. The many gods were flawed, imperfect, and cruel; they cheated on their wives, they cursed anyone who didn't cater to their vanity, they argued and fought and loved. They acted like people. But people are fuck-ups. Why would you worship anyone who reminded you of yourself?

And so eventually we came to the One God, the Perfect God, the Omnipotent, Omniscient, Omnibenevolent God, the God who sits over and above all of our human bullshit. We grew into that – or we stayed savages, and savages didn't count as humans anymore. You could kill them or convert – or, like as not, one after the other.

Plato knew that the beautiful, eternal truth of his God was the natural evolution of human belief. We would all end up there eventually. Whether the crusaders came with chainmail and swords or smiles and purple sweaters, they knew that, if they knew that, if they just pressed you hard enough and long enough, one day, you would break down and let yourself be saved.

But the One True God didn't do a goddamned thing for Jimmy, or for Grimey. And I'll be damned before I let him do a thing for me.

I stood there with the concrete hunk in my hand, thinking long and hard about what I was about to do.

I had to put something in order first. I took out my phone, dialed her number. Let it ring. Once, twice—

"Hello?" Lucy said. "Lou?"

"Hey, Luce," I said, softly.

"What's going on? I'm sorry, I lost my charger, I only just got your message this morning…"

"That's alright. It doesn't really matter now," I said. "I just need to tell you something."

"Is it about the other weekend? Look, I've wanted to talk to you about it, but…"

"No, it's not about that." I swallowed. "Look, I need to be quick about this. It might be a while before you see me again. I'm not sure what I'm going to be like the next time you do. Just trust me. I'm calling you to tell you that this was the right thing to do."

"That *what* is the right thing to do? I don't understand."

I felt the rock in my hand, that imperfect rock, that imperfect hand. Nobody would understand this. I suppose I didn't really understand it myself. *Dr. Eccleston is such a kind man, gentle, patient,* they'll say. *Such a nice man.* They will never understand how that only makes it worse.

My arm swung back, and then the rock was gone.

Things went slowly then. I could see the chunk of concrete, see it darting upward, could see gravity pull it into an inexorable falling arc. Nothing to be done about it anymore. It was out of my hands. Sometimes you make a decision, and you don't know what's going to happen, but you know it's too late to do anything but wait for the consequences. Sometimes it feels like my whole life has been that way...

The window pane shattered under the impact of the rock. The frame buckled, and each shard of glass crashed away, exactly like frenzied wind chimes. Sunlight danced in the cracks of the remaining glass, and within seconds, everything was still and silent once more.

"Lou? Lou, what the fuck was that?" Lucy cried into the phone.

"A choice," I said. "Bye Lucy. I love you."

"Wait, what? Lou, you son of a bitch, don't—"

And I hung up.

Soon, there would be yelling, and chases, and handcuffs. I was sure of that. Kirksville was too small a town to get away with anything. But they would have to catch me first. I walked out of the alley, back into the sunlight.

The sun caught on something shining, silver, at my feet. I picked it up: a U.S. quarter, minted in 1976.

The quarter hit the sidewalk with a clink, and I ran until I heard the sirens.

MOON
BOOKS

Moon Books invites you to begin or deepen your encounter with Paganism, in all its rich, creative, flourishing forms.